SAPIENT CURSE

SPELLCREST ACADEMY, BOOK 7

MICHAEL PIERCE

CHAPTER 1

"We are gathered here today to remember our Spellcrest brothers and sisters, all of the students, faculty, and residents we lost to the vampires one year ago." Headmistress Christi stood before the whole student body—though we still didn't have the numbers from before the plague vampires had tried to claim us as their own—atop the steps of the Manor, numerous professors positioned behind her. My mother was among them.

"It's hard to believe it has already been so long," the headmistress continued, speaking through a cordless microphone. "To many of us, the horrific events that threatened to destroy our institution seemed like only yesterday. But we endured. We continue to heal. And we are stronger for it.

"We lost many brave souls during those long,

dark weeks—among the darkest hours this academy has ever seen. They may be gone, but they are not forgotten. Nor will they ever be."

I glanced over at Nym, seeing what those dark weeks had produced. Our *little elf* had died during the battle, but she wasn't completely taken from us.

However, a part of her still hadn't returned—and God only knew if it ever would.

I was never one to give up hope. Some would have called me annoyingly persistent. But the real Nym was inside the gorgeous vampire body somewhere.

We were all gathered in the back of the crowd, Nym still not overly comfortable in large groups. Through all the evil shit, our neophyte crew had stuck together.

And we were far from neophytes anymore. We were starting the second trimester of our sapient year—the first day back to school after the holiday break.

Razielle and I kept Nym between us.

Ivanic was always at Razielle's side. On my right were Sarah and Erik, who had broken up again last summer, but were determined to make it last this time. Bree stood at the far end of the group, whispering something in Sarah's ear only Nym would have the ability to hear.

Finley remained a year behind me. He was now living in Rainley Hall and had the pleasure of enduring Intro to Evocation with our mother. His embarrassment was obvious every time I brought it up. But I saw less of him during the school year, allowing him more space to live his own life.

Aside from crossing paths on campus, the most I saw of him was at family dinners on Sundays, the one time during the week we'd all convene around the same kitchen table and inform the rest of the family what was going on in our lives.

The normal stuff, now that we could call our new magical lives *normal*. This wasn't for friends and significant others. Just our semi-nuclear family unit, which had expanded to include Quin.

"Let us bow our heads and have a moment of silence for those we lost last year," Headmistress Christi said.

The snow-covered area in which we were all gathered instantly quieted of errant chatter.

The constant breeze and chirping of birds were the only remaining sounds while we all stood with lowered heads.

It only took a few seconds for the whispers and snickers of a few nearby neophytes to reach my ears. They didn't have the respect the rest of us had for this solemn gathering because they hadn't been here last year, hadn't lived through what the rest of us had.

A couple of years ago, I would have been the one to smack them in the back of the head, but was learning not to start fights at every urge—and God knew my urges were plentiful.

When the headmistress began talking again, I turned my attention from the irritating neophytes back to her. The first time I'd seen her since returning from the dead was in this very spot. She was standing beside me as Chairman Blackwater was making his official announcement that Spellcrest Academy belonged to him and the rest of the plague vampires—the Vampire Order. And now the headmistress was on the stage, assuring us we'd never have to live through something so dark again. This was a new age. A better Spellcrest. And that we all had hopeful futures.

I sure hope you're right.

The fight with the plague vampires had become known as the Battle of Spellcrest, superseding the previous battle against Tarquin's army when the vampires had first been released.

The school had withstood two battles in the two years I'd been attending, and I tried to look at it as nothing more than a strange coincidence.

I couldn't honestly believe I was the common factor here—the bad omen—though I did question the possibility on way too many nights while lying awake in bed.

"As we start this new year and a new trimester, I task you all with making the most of your time here and all Spellcrest Academy has to offer," Headmistress Christi said. "Your professors and I will do everything we can to prepare you for all the luxuries and challenges that lie ahead for you as magicals. One way of making sure your fellow students will never be forgotten—to honor their memories— is to take advantage of your time here. Do not let a single moment go to waste. Learn. Do. Grow. And go forth and contribute to an ever-expanding world.

"Whenever you feel your motivation and gratitude begin to wane, I have one more thing for you. Something to help you remember how blessed and special you are. And I want you all to follow me and see it for yourselves—the newly completed Spellcrest Academy Memorial Hall."

The headmistress waved us forward, urging the gathered study body to ascend the steps of the Manor. The professors at the top of the stairs remained on each side of the main entrance as the headmistress passed through the glass doors.

"Where is she taking us?" Razielle asked. "Is the Manor now Memorial Hall?"

"You think *I* know?" I answered.

"Well, your mom's up there. You're like besties with the headmistress, and you're practically engaged to her son. So, yeah, I expect you to have some insider information."

"I'm glad you think so highly of my connections," I laughed. "But I know nothing. And just because I don't think the headmistress hates me anymore, I'm certainly not *besties* with her."

"Good, because I can't compete with the likes of her."

"I think I'm gonna go back to the room," Nym said.

"I second that," Erik said, grabbing Sarah by the waist.

"Oh, come on, aren't you the slightest bit curious?" I asked. "I'm sure a lot of work went into what the headmistress wants to show us."

"You *do* know something!" Razielle said, accusatorily.

"I don't! I swear! I'm just saying…"

"I'm not saying I never want to see it," Nym said. "Just not right now with the whole campus. I'll come with you later—like, after lunch or something."

"Don't worry, little elf. We're all here to protect you," I said with a smile.

"I'm not worried about that." Her *I'm not amused* glare had become absolutely killer.

"Then we're all here to protect everyone else from you." I was about to put a hand on her shoulder, then remembered her new stance on physical contact, and instead stuffed my hand into the pocket of my leather jacket. "We're in the back. We'll *remain* in the back. We're not in the middle of the herd. Think of it as an extra training session."

"We can all go later," Sarah said.

Nym kept her focus on me, almost turning it into a staring contest. I wasn't trying to win, but thought this would be good for her. I knew better than to push her too hard. It may have been a year, but she was still adjusting to her new life as a vampire.

She was still getting used to her abilities, still transforming.

As much as we thought she'd immediately *been* transformed, which shouldn't have been possible for someone her age, we later realized it hadn't been complete.

I didn't know exactly what the plague vampires had done with turning a number of students. They were ravenous and vampire-like, but weren't fully transitioned vampires.

They could still go out in sunlight. They could still taste regular food.

Their compulsion to kill was not the same as the growing compulsion for blood.

Now, those curses of her condition were taking effect.

She was feeling as if she was going through it alone, even though there were eleven other newly turned vampires and three additional transitioning ones at the Academy. We tried to be there for her as much as possible, but there was only so much we could do. The biggest help came from the support group the headmistress formed to help guide the Academy's growing vampire population. This took the place of her magical concentration elective this school year.

"I'll go," Nym finally said, getting groans from Erik and Sarah even though no one was forcing them to come.

"If we milk this long enough, then we won't have to go back to our first periods," Ivanic said. "Starting the day off with Multi-World History is just torture. How is anyone supposed to stay awake in that class at eight o'clock in the morning?"

"Are you able to stay awake in any first-period class?" Razielle chided. "You're practically nocturnal."

"Well, at least we have another nocturnal member of the group."

"*I'm* not nocturnal," Nym said. "I can still stand the sun… at least for a little while. And I'm going to bask in it for as long as I can."

Enough of the students ahead of us had begun to move, opening a rift between us and the rest of the school. We were in no hurry to follow, determined to social distance for Nym's sake. But after a few more minutes, we were climbing the front steps of the Manor. Each of us greeted Mom as we passed, along with a few other professors we'd had over the past few years.

The procession of students continued past the interior staircase. The hallway we were about to enter had its overhead lights dimmed.

I could already make out glowing markings and pictures on each wall ahead, becoming even more radiant in the dimmed light.

"What is this?" Razielle asked, though I couldn't tell if she truly expected an answer.

No one did. We entered the picturesque hallway in awe at what decorated the walls. Entire sections of the hallway had been dedicated to different students.

A stylized name popped from the wall from glowing blue letters, as bright and shimmering as the wound of an open seam. And positioned around the name was a multitude of pictures and short videos on loops, making the student come alive from the hallway wall.

I didn't recognize most names, but did know several familiar faces from passing those students on campus or in the dorms.

The hallway turned a corner, continuing with the memorial. During this stretch of remembrances, a familiar name did jump out at me—Yana Everest. She had been Nym's combative casting partner for a time back when we were neophytes, when Professor Windsor wanted to shake things up and make sure we didn't get too comfortable. It seemed like so long ago and we had shared other classes since then, but it was her becoming Nym's partner that cemented her name in my memory.

I glanced over at Nym to find her transfixed on a looping video of Yana magically playing on the wall.

"How are you doing?" I asked.

Razielle and Ivanic stopped beside us while the others continued slowly down the hall.

"I remember seeing her in the catacombs," Nym said. "She was so scared—they all were."

"It's not your fault."

"Except I think it was... I think *I* was the one who killed her."

She couldn't pry her eyes away from the wall.

"It's *not* your fault," I repeated. "It's the fault of those plague vampire bastards. You weren't in control of your actions. You're just as much a victim as everyone else on these walls."

"I hear what you're saying, but I still did it. It doesn't matter whether or not I'd be found guilty in a court of law. It doesn't matter if I could claim insanity. Her death—and the deaths of others—were still at my hand."

"This wasn't supposed to be a walk down guilt-trip lane." I hadn't thought about Nym as one of the killers, and about how that would have affected her, seeing all these names and faces. We were all grieving, but her grief was from a different perspective.

"Maybe this was a bad idea after all," Razielle said, and I was starting to agree.

"Are you guys coming?" Bree called back to us from the next turn in the hallway.

"Come on," I said to urge Nym away from the collage of her former class partner. "I'm sorry I forced you to do this."

"You didn't force me," Nym said, but she finally started walking again.

As she continued, she still oscillated her attention from wall to wall, making sure not to miss a single name, but at least she didn't stop.

The rest of our group waited for us to catch up, then we headed down the last stretch of hallway together, finishing the u-shape and leading us back to the main entrance of the Manor.

However, Nym didn't make it halfway down this hallway before stopping again. When the rest of us saw what had captured her attention, we came to a crashing halt too.

Nym Uriro. No...

An unbelievable montage of her first two years at the Academy took up a wide section of the wall. I didn't even know where these pictures and videos had come from. It wasn't as if I'd provided any of them. From the looks of horror consuming the rest of our friend group, I couldn't imagine anyone else having supplied these images of our sweet, undead friend.

But we were *all* there, immortalized on this wall.

There was a picture of the seven of us in the cafeteria, posed from someone taking our picture. Another of us as roommates with Finley and

Grayson, obviously early in our first year. Then more of the three of us in our dorm rooms.

Who the hell's taking these pictures?

"I'm not dead," Nym said quietly, almost sounding like her old self for a moment.

"We know," I said. "There must be some mistake."

I'd been conscious of not touching her since she'd been turned, but didn't hesitate to grab her arm now. "Please, Nym. Let's get out of here."

"I'm not dead!" she repeated, louder this time. She shook my hand off her arm and clawed at the pictures on the wall, but they were somehow embedded into the finish, so there was nothing for her to tear down. Nym raked her nails down the wall, leaving gashes in the paint, but the pictures and videos remained mostly unharmed.

Nym's outburst got the attention of the few remaining students at the end of the hall and a few professors standing by the Manor entrance.

Then Mom pushed past a cluster of students and was running toward us, concern etched upon her face. When she reached the memorial to everyone's favorite elf, her eyes widened even more.

"Oh, honey... I can't believe they did this," Mom gasped and pulled Nym into her.

Strangely enough, Nym didn't fight but folded into her, practically on the verge of tears. I wanted to put a hand on her back, but my hesitation got the best of me again. Nym had become more comfortable with my mother than me.

"I was afraid everyone thought of me as dead…" Nym cried. "Now I know it's true."

Mom pushed Nym back to look her straight in the eyes. "It's *not* true. You're the same amazing girl I met before this happened. But the most important thing is that *you* need to believe it, which I know will take time. Luckily, time is something you have in abundance." Mom gave her an encouraging smile. "Let's get you out of here."

CHAPTER 2

*I*t seemed as though I was always apologizing to Nym for something, and the start of this new year was no different.

While other students were heading back to finish first period, Nym, Razielle, and I returned to our room for a breather. Razielle and I shared Divination, so if one of us was going to skip, then we might as well both skip. Or maybe it should have been the opposite and one of us should have gone. Whatever, our roommate needed us.

Mom was able to work her magic at the beginning of the school year, and the three of us would be able to room together for one more year. The head of Shadow Peaks Hall, Professor Ocumulus, wasn't thrilled with the idea of all three of us crammed into one room. But he also didn't want to be responsible for pairing up one of the new vampires with another student.

So, we were together again—and I wouldn't want it any other way. However, Nym was more particular about her space these days. She claimed the single bed, leaving Razielle and me to negotiate the bunk arrangements. Since Razielle had never slept on a top bunk, I let her have it with a simple flip of a coin I manipulated into losing.

"I can't show my face around here anymore," Nym cried as she dropped onto her bed. "But what am I supposed to do? It's not as though my parents want me home anytime soon—if ever."

"It was stupid and insensitive," I said, sitting across the room from her.

Razielle grabbed one of the desk chairs. "I'm sure it will come up in your vampire acclimation class. The others must be just as hurt as you. If you all petition to the headmistress, you can probably get your names removed."

"That's not the point," Nym said. "The school has already shown how they truly feel. We're literally dead to them."

"You're still enrolled, aren't you?"

"Like how my mother said she didn't know, maybe it's only a select few school officials who worked on the project, so it's not representative of how the administration as a whole thinks," I said. "But maybe

"I say we should celebrate with getting some decadent food while you can still enjoy it," Razielle motioned. "I'm all about the waffles this morning. Who's in?"

"Don't you have Advanced Evo next?" I asked.

"What's one more free period for a girl in need?"

Nym didn't look so sure.

"You girls do what you want," I said. "I shouldn't miss History. And my work here is done."

"Thanks, Maeve. Thanks to you both," Nym said, pushing back up into a seated position. "I'm all for getting extra dessert this afternoon. The sweeter the better."

"*Fine,*" Razielle said grudgingly.

"Count me in," I said. Her taste buds weren't as discerning as they used to be, so she needed the more extreme flavors for them to still register.

From what I'd heard, she wouldn't be enjoying food for much longer. Her transition to blood hadn't begun, but the urge was already starting. It was the part everyone was afraid of.

I vividly remembered being around her in the early days of her transformation and how ravenous and consumed she'd been. It had a lot to do with special magic the plague vampires cast upon her, which was now gone, but her state at the time was still a sobering precursor of what was to come when Nym reached maturity and fully transformed into a vampire.

I didn't fear for myself around her, but feared for my friend.

Since Razielle couldn't convince Nym to ditch another class, the three of us headed back to the Manor together. It was strange walking toward the gothic building and not seeing the lonely tower in the distance. It had been such a staple of the skyline, and now it was gone.

Razielle and Nym headed upstairs to Advanced Evocation while I turned to a non-memorial hall-way, headed for Multi-World History with Professor Haricot.

She was a frail, bronzed, and leathery-skinned woman with permed bluish-white hair and narrow glasses. She loved that I was in her class, with me being a seamstress and I would one day travel to many of the worlds mentioned in the textbook. It was as if she wanted to be my Spellcrest-appointed travel agent.

I shared this class with Sarah and Erik, making a line out of the last row. I got there first, but didn't have to save their seats. Everyone had come to expect they were ours. I only had to instruct a fellow sapient to keep walking once early last trimester. Since then, no one else had even tried to claim one of our seats.

"Now that we've scratched the surface of a few known and explored worlds, we'll do a deeper dive this trimester into one I know you're all relatively familiar with—Kicryria. It is a magical world with a rich history, which I know you'll find fascinating."

My heart leapt at the thought of learning more about my father's home planet. His blood and the blood of his people ran through my veins. And besides my few short trips there, including the one to my grandparent's house and the beautiful skyline of Ylagos in the distance, I didn't know much about the world, its people, or its history. My father had talked about it briefly since he'd been back, but not the kind of information that would compare to a history course unit.

"Who would like to tell me an interesting fact about Kicryria?" Professor Haricot asked.

Immediately, several hands went up, but mine wasn't one.

As much as I wanted to learn about the world, I was afraid to reveal what I already knew about it—as well as my connection to it, unsure of what the professor already knew about me.

Sure, it was clear I was a seamstress, but did she know I was half-Kicryrian, not something I admitted to the whole student body?

"We've been at war with them since the seventies," said the first student Professor Haricot called on.

"1973 by our records," she said. "But that was something we briefly covered last trimester. Anyone have an interesting fact from something we *haven't* covered?"

Several hands went down, but a few remained.

"There are over thirty dialects of Kicranese, but it is the official language of the Kicryrian people," a girl named Milani said. "The planet it about a fourth the size of Earth and the civilizations are not as broken up as they are here. They all reside under one central government."

"All true statements," Professor Haricot said.

While a few more students shared, I thought of something I could say without revealing too much about myself.

As the final student shared, I shot my hand up.

The professor's attention turned to me, her lips curling into a smile. "Yes, Miss Maeve? And what would you like to add?"

"Kicryria has spiders that are like ten times the size of tarantulas," I said. "Their bite temporarily paralyzes you. And their web hinders magical abilities."

"Really? Now that's one I haven't heard before," she said with a thoughtful expression. More than a few students had turned in their chairs to look at me. "Where did you learn about these giant spiders?"

"I saw them… and killed a few. Their blood is black and thick like tar."

"You've actually been to Kicryria?"

I wasn't sure if it was a good idea to answer this

question truthfully, so I instead told the truth about where I'd seen them. "I ran into them here—in Spell-crest Village—when the Kicyrians were attacking two years ago. My mother was with me, and she knew what they were."

"I see. So many things in such a short period of time we'd all like to forget," Professor Haricot said. "I trust none of them survived that night. I wouldn't want to run into any giant spiders."

She shivered at the mere thought of the hairy abominations.

Too bad I didn't have pictures to show the class.

Professor Haricot moved on to her planned lesson, and I remained more alert than usual in history class—any history class.

CHAPTER 3

*A*fter Multi-World History, I bid farewell to the original lovebirds of the group and headed to Non-Magical Studies. It was still primarily review for me, not that I wanted to put much focus and energy into this class anyway. I wasn't in the premier magical academy in the country to learn about Trigonometry and Chemistry. Where were those classes going to get me anyway? I was here to learn how to harness my innate magical abilities. Non-Magical Studies should be an elective. But if it was, who in their right mind would take it?

And it wasn't just us. The professor didn't even want to be here. Professor Thumri looked about as bored as I was feeling. The class wasn't just lacking magical energy, it was lacking any energy whatsoever. I suspected the professor's assignment to this class was a punishment.

I ran to grab a coffee before heading to Advanced Evocation, needing the caffeine jolt. This was considered a lab class with shared tables. I partnered with Bree, and the boys claimed the table behind us. Now that Ivanic was with Razielle, he essentially detached himself from me, which I didn't complain about. I never would have thought I'd start missing his suggestive comments and innuendos, but a small part of me did.

"Rough hour in NMS?" Bree asked, how some of the students referred to Non-Magical Studies.

"I needed to slap myself a few times," I said between literal chugs of coffee. Luckily, I'd put enough creamer in to make it lukewarm.

"At least you don't have it first period."

"We get it over with right off the bat," Ivanic said from the table behind us.

"Not today," Erik added. "It was glorious!"

"It'll be back to normal tomorrow," I said, which was Divination for me. Not so bad.

"*Can't wait.*"

This class was taught by Professor Quail, who was supposed to have been our original Intro to Evocation professor, the class that my mother had taken over last year. With her back and still teaching, Professor Quail moved up to Advanced Evocation.

Razielle had mentioned not liking him when he'd

taken over the class last year while my mother was in a GBMA prison, but it had more to do with his grating voice than his actual personality or teaching style. He certainly wasn't someone you'd want to listen to through a guided meditation, but I didn't hold anything against the guy.

In Advanced Evocation, we'd moved beyond the introductory tasks of stealing pencils and manifesting our names onto the whiteboard, now attempting to conjure real items and coax them into the physical plane.

Last trimester, we started small by conjuring—what else—but a pencil. But this wasn't moving a pencil from one box to another. This was envisioning a pencil from a picture in your mind and creating it out of thin air.

As always, focus and concentration were key. But now, attention to detail was equally important. A vague picture of a pencil would not create a pencil. And a pencil was about as basic of an item to envision.

Unlike most of the other students, I had gotten quite a bit of practice with producing clear pictures for teleporting, learning to harness one of my non-exclusive seamstress gifts. This gave me a leg up with manifesting, which I hadn't previously realized how similar the abilities were—with teleporting being more advanced.

So, with my extra practice, my octagram tattoo,

and my soul crystal warming my chest, I was back to making the assignments look easy.

Bree was better at this than Infusions, but she still leaned on me for help.

However, today we were starting something completely different, but something else that immediately got my attention.

"Today you will reach into your partner's mind," Professor Quail said, standing at the front of the class. "Just like reaching for an object you can't currently see, you'll now be reaching for a thought, which can be just as elusive. Thoughts, like energy, are all around you. And similar to energy, you're continually passing through them like the air you breathe. You're not conscious of their proximity until you still, quiet, and listen closely. The greatest masters of this skill can practically see the words floating through the air—and all those masters have to do is read them as they pass."

I believed this was the skill that Mom and Quin had used to get through to Finley while his lips were sewn shut. I'd tried everything to reach him—having him write or text—but the magical binding on him wouldn't allow him to do either. He was silenced as much as a person could be. However, this was how Mom and Quin had ultimately reached him, and if I remembered correctly, they'd attributed the skill to this class.

As I felt heat at my chest from the crystal, in which Tarquin's soul still hung in limbo, I was also reminded of how he could project his voice into my head, bypassing his magical binding. These skills were probably two sides to the same coin.

"I'm sure you're wondering how you're going to confirm what you're hearing is correct," Professor Quail added. "Well, it's quite simple. You'll each write a message on a piece of paper, but don't allow your partner to see what you've written. Keep it simple. I'd suggest starting with a single word. Then you will fold the paper and recite the message in your mind. Your intention will be focused on your partner. Block out any other noise you begin to hear. Listen for the closest mantra—your partner continuing to recite the message in his or her mind. When you think you have it, then reveal what you've heard to your partner. What's written on the paper will confirm or reject your answer. Let us begin."

Two students seated at the front of the class passed out sheets of paper to the rest of us.

"Please make it easy for me," Bree said once we had our papers. "He said it could be one word. Let's do that."

"Sounds good to me," I said. "Easy, but not something you'd immediately think of."

"I can't say there's one word I'd fully associate with you."

"I can think of a few," Erik said, sarcastically.

"And there's your problem," I said. "*A few*. But which one describes me best?"

"Stubborn."

"Good, then I won't use that one."

"Pain in the ass?"

"Also not one word," I said.

"But it's a single descriptor, so I'd say it counts."

Erik received an elbow from Ivanic. "Don't call the godmother to my future cubs that."

"Now I'm a godmother, am I? Like a fairy godmother?" I laughed.

"Shut up, you guys. I can't think," Bree complained. "I need to come up with a good word."

"You can literally choose any word you want," Erik said. "It doesn't have to be relevant to your partner. In fact, it's probably better if it isn't." He quickly jotted something on the paper in front of him, hiding his word from view with his opposite arm. "There. Done."

I agreed with Erik's assessment, but wanted to make my word relevant to Bree to hopefully make it easier for her. But I didn't want to overthink it. After taking another ten seconds for myself, I scribbled my word and folded the paper into quarters.

"Are you ready?" I asked Bree.

"Almost…" she said, staring blankly toward the front of the classroom. The paper before her remained blank. "This is *so* hard."

I was tempted to tell her this was literally the easiest part of the exercise, but held my tongue. No use in stressing her out more.

"Magic. Homework. Tired. Chicken. Thirteen. Blue. Idaho. Boobs—" Erik said.

"Are you just rattling off every word that comes into your head?" Ivanic asked.

"Yup."

"Shut up," Bree said.

"Boobs? Really?" I scolded.

"Good one, right? You'd never have guessed it coming from Bree," Erik said, sounding incredibly proud of himself. "And I was picturing Sarah's. Not that you girls don't have nice racks, but I have respect for my friends."

"Sure, you do." I rolled my eyes, and when I glanced over at Bree, I discovered she was finally writing. "Is it a hard one?" I could feel the eyes of the guys behind us as soon as I said it, but wasn't about to take it back.

"I guess we'll see," Bree said and folded her paper. "Do you want to go first?"

"No pressure." I looked around to see how other students were fairing. The room was mostly quiet now. Professor Quail was circulating to each desk to give guidance and pointers.

I'm looking for a word.

I listened to the silence, but kept hearing the professor's voice, even though he was talking quietly. And with a voice like his—even with him speaking barely above a whisper—it was hard to block it out. If I was having so much trouble, I couldn't imagine Nym trying to drown him out.

"Anything?" Bree asked.

"Not when you're interrupting my Zen," I said, only half-joking.

"Sorry. I didn't know how long I was supposed to wait."

"Until I give you an answer or say I give up," I said and shut my eyes, trying harder to tune out everything around me. But as I tried to focus on a single word emerging from the depths, all I could hear was Erik talking about boobs. The more I tried not to think of the word, the more it fought to remain in the forefront of my mind.

"How are we doing over here?" Professor Quail said, now suddenly standing before our table.

"Not good," I said, exasperated. "Erik made a comment early, and now the only word I keep hearing is *boobs*. Maybe I'm picking up on his word."

I thought Bree would have laughed at my admission of failure, but she only looked defeated as she unfolded her paper—and on it was written the word *boobs*.

"That's not really classroom appropriate, Miss Nelson," Professor Quail said, looking down at her paper. However, he looked more uncomfortable than upset.

"You actually wrote that?" I asked, shocked.

"You took one of my suggestions?" Erik laughed.

"It seemed a good idea at the time," Bree said. "Like you said, it would be so unlike something I'd write on my own."

"But not so unlike Maeve to guess it."

"Vulgarity aside, nice work," Professor Quail said. "I hope the word you've written is more appropriate, Miss Rainley."

"I plead the fifth," I said with a devious smile, clapping my palm over the folded paper. "I shall give nothing away."

"But you have," Ivanic said. "You've given everything away! I know where the poison is!"

I snorted laughter at his *Princess Bride* reference, then glanced over at Bree who didn't look any more confident.

"Carry on," Professor Quail said, leaving the lot of us to our questioningly appropriate shenanigans.

I turned my full attention to Bree, keeping one hand on my confidential paper. "You can do it, Bree. Listen closely and hear what I'm sending your way."

"Are you doing it now?" Bree asked.

"Yup. But you can't listen if you're talking."

"Right," Bree said, her eyes widening as she stared at me as if she was searching out blemishes on my face. Even though that wasn't going to help, I tried not to break her creepy concentration, kind of wanting to blow in her face just to make her blink.

The sounds of celebration from the boys behind us didn't help Bree retain her focus.

"Crap, I'm not getting anything," Bree said. "But that's not something you'd say. You'd say *shit*." Then her eyes lit up. "Is that it? Is that your word? Since you were saying you were hearing boobs so much, now it's all I'm hearing too. Did you end up choosing that word too?"

"I dunno," I said. "Which is it? Shit or boobs?"

The table behind us suddenly got very quiet.

Bree looked as if she was on the hook for the million-dollar question. "I don't know. They're both reverberating in my head."

"Boobs are always reverberating in my head," Erik said.

"Shut up, horndog," I scolded. "Let the girl think. Shit or boobs?"

"Boobs," Bree said with a sigh.

"Is that your final answer?"

"Yes?" Her answer squeaked out as a question, but I took it.

"You got me," I said. "Two girls with boobs."

"I knew it!" Ivanic exclaimed, causing more laughter from Erik.

I unfolded my paper and revealed the *boobs*, even though I hadn't originally written the word on my paper. I was just thankful I'd successfully pulled off the magical sleight of hand. And the elation on Bree's face made the gamble worth it.

"I did it!" Her smile was so wide it looked painful.

Erik crumpled his paper into a ball and chucked it at Ivanic. "Damn, we should have picked better words."

CHAPTER 4

"You wouldn't believe how these girls were behaving in Advanced Evo," Ivanic said to Razielle once we were all seated in the cafeteria. "They were putting us boys to shame."

"When Maeve's involved? Yeah, I can believe it," Razielle said and gave me a smirk. "But what did she do this time?"

"We were talking about boobs," Bree chimed in, sounding so very proud of herself. She was still running on a dopamine high from her success in the previous class—at least in *her* mind. "You know, typical girl talk."

"I see." Razielle tried to coax the silly grin off her boyfriend's face, but he couldn't help himself. Neither could Erik.

We'd all had a little too much fun in Advance

SAPIENT CURSE

Evocation. It was obvious Razielle was feeling left out, wishing she was sharing the class with us too, but she'd had it with Nym earlier in the morning. Probably, there weren't as many shenanigans happening in their class.

"I'm glad *you guys* had fun," Sarah said. "Combative Casting was *not* such a walk in the park. I got nightmares from it last trimester, and that was the easy stuff."

"I'm already trying to block it out," Bree said. "At least Advanced Evo cheered me up."

"A lot of us have it next," Razielle said. I was in the same class, along with Nym and Erik. "Any pointers?"

"Vampires aren't restricted content anymore," Ivanic said, nervously glancing at Nym.

Nym didn't react to the news, continuing to pick at her food. She'd never been a heavy eater like Razielle, but her interest in food was waning with her taste buds.

"I guess the powers that be feel we can handle it now," I said. "Nym, what do you think?"

"They don't scare me anymore," she said. "But I guess it will depend on how they portray them."

"Or how *you* portray them. I'm sure the experience will be different for all of us."

"Yes. I'm supposed to view them as kin, and you're supposed to view them as the enemy."

"That's not entirely true."

35

"But it's true enough."

I didn't want to perpetuate the disagreement, so I let it go. "Look at what we've already been through— lived through. The Academy's simulations aren't going to crack us."

"Though you might not want to eat too much before going in there," Ivanic added. "Mine got pretty gnarly today."

"Good pointer."

"Are you allowed to transform yet?" Razielle asked.

Ivanic shook his head. "It's not fair. Nym will be able to use all her abilities, but I'm not allowed to take advantage of mine."

"Because you're not yourself when you're a cougar," Nym said. "It's different. You'd probably break the machine."

"Yeah, but it still sucks." Ivanic ripped into a chicken strip, then dunked the torn end in ketchup before tossing it into his mouth.

"Sounds like we have a lot to look forward to," I said, now that everyone was successfully depressed.

The table was quiet for a few minutes. Now, more of us than just Nym was picking at our food. After Ivanic's suggestion, I'd be throwing most of mine away. What made it even more frustrating was how delicious my fish tacos were.

"What did the rest of you think about the new TA in Divination?" Ivanic asked breaking the silence.

"She seemed nice," Nym said. "I think she said she's still attending Concordia University, so she's only here half days. I guess the headmistress is helping her travel."

"Yeah, she's from somewhere in Canada. But did she tell your class she's a wolf shifter?"

"She mentioned it."

"She didn't really say anything in the limited time we were in first period," Sarah said. "She was just getting situated."

"You went back to class after the memorial?" Razielle asked.

"Yeah. I wasn't invited to ditch with you girls."

She sounded somewhat bitter, but then again, hadn't asked to tag along. It wasn't as if we would have turned her down. We had just been more focused on Nym.

"Sorry," I said. "It wasn't exactly planned."

"That's okay. At least I didn't get an incomplete for the day, like you three."

"I'll have my mother write us a note."

"And here we go again with the connections. First, it was Devon, now it's your mother."

"You saw what they did," I argued. "We had a valid excuse." I looked at Nym, then at Razielle before returning my gaze to Sarah. "But there's no reason we can't take our marks like adults."

"I don't need your mother to write a note for me,"

Razielle said. "I'll tell Professor Lin straight up why we didn't come back."

"Then we're good," I said. "Are *we* good, Sarah?"

She sighed. "Yeah. But don't make a habit of leaving me out."

She was starting to sound like Razielle complaining about me ditching her in dangerous situations—something she still reminded me of whenever she got the chance.

"*I* thought it was cool that Miss Long was a wolf shifter," Ivanic said. Now he was the one who sounded bitter. "And she went here only a few years ago. She's not much older than us. I forgot when she said she graduated."

"The year before we started," Nym said. "You're so infatuated with the fact she's a shifter, you literally didn't hear anything else."

"Is she pretty?" Razielle asked, sounding increasingly concerned.

"I don't know," Ivanic said, trying to get out from under the spotlight of his girlfriend's glare. "I wasn't really looking at her."

"Don't look at me. I'm not answering that question," Erik said, receiving approval from Sarah.

"I feel like I'm being objective with saying she's gorgeous," Nym said, and Bree nodded.

"*Fantastic*," Razielle groaned. "My cougar is going to chase after a wolf."

"I am not. You've got nothing to worry about,

Raz," Ivanic insisted. "I just haven't met many shifters here, so I thought it was noteworthy."

"And it also doesn't help that you have a thing for older women—no offense, Maeve."

"None taken," I said. "You better watch yourself, cougar boy. If you hurt my friend, you'll have to deal with both of us."

"Make it three," Nym said.

"And you don't want to see our vampire elf angry." I grinned widely. His discomfort brought back fond memories of freshman year—well, freshman year *here*. The happy times when my brother hadn't betrayed me and a Kicryrian lieutenant hadn't been trying to kill me.

I could feel the warmth in my chest from the mere thought of Tarquin.

He could have been trying to poke me with a red-hot iron for all I knew, though what I was feeling was a spreading warmth from sipping a steaming coffee.

The lunch hour finished with half of us tossing most of our food in the trash.

It might have been wasteful, but wasn't something we did often. The boys were even known for scarfing down some of our leftovers, but not today.

Erik was in Combative Casting with Razielle, Nym, and me. Ivanic was having a hard time recovering from Razielle's accusations of him having the hots for the new TA in Divination.

I was sure Razielle would be judging her intently tomorrow morning, and I'd be dragged right into the pool of paranoia. However, everything I knew about Ivanic from the past few years was pointing to him being extraordinarily loyal. So as Ivanic had said, Razielle should have nothing to worry about. At least, *I* wasn't worried.

The four of us headed to Shadow Peaks Hall, where the Combative Casting Three class was held. It was a large room in the basement, not far from where I'd found the plague vampire staff hidden in the floor last year. From my adequately honed needle-sensing abilities, the magical artifact hadn't been returned to that office.

"It's not gonna be so bad, right?" Razielle asked as we neared the classroom. However, it was more than just a single classroom. It was a large laboratory with individual pods equipped for virtual reality simulations. This class was nothing like the iterations of the last two years.

"You're building it up in your head," I said. "You'll make it as bad as it's going to be."

"Bree survived," Erik said. "If she can handle it, then I'm sure you can do it."

"Bree might be more fearful, but I've experienced more things to be afraid of," Razielle said.

And therein lay the effectiveness and horror of the simulations.

They had been developing a personalized baseline for each student's experience, imagination, and fears. The simulations started with preprogramed scenarios, starting everyone at the same point—a safe room where we could feel comfortable. But we each created the world outside the room as the simulations continued, then conjured the enemies that inhabited it.

Everyone was scarred by something, but I carried many scars with me.

I hadn't yet met my demons, but they were in there, loaded into the almighty computer, ready to strike once the parameters of the simulation were increased. This would happen once the baseline was fully established, which was completed before we left for winter break.

Today would be the first time navigating the world—or Hell—we each created without parental controls or training wheels. This would be as close to the real thing as we'd come in a controlled schooling environment. You might have known it was a simulation going in, but once you were there —in the fabricated world of your own creation—the simulation faded from your mind, and you were actually there. This wasn't like wearing an Oculus VR headset.

This was a full-body sensory experience more vivid than real life.

I had no idea where the technology came from— or when, for that matter. We weren't given any training or history on the simulator itself. We simply entered our pods when we were told and did our best to remind ourselves what we were about to experience wasn't real.

Something told me we'd be repeating the mantra even more so today.

We entered the laboratory behind another small group of students. The air was thick with anxiety and fearful anticipation. By this point in the day, we all knew what was coming. We were told what was coming last trimester, but now, we all had friends who'd experienced the unrestrained simulations. And that news had obviously spread like an incoming storm.

"Welcome back, lab rats," Professor Ocumulus boomed once the clock struck one. He had a sense of humor as dry as a desert carcass. At least I thought it was dry humor. Otherwise, he was just mean. "I hope you had a pleasant holiday."

All this man's features were hairy and large, most of his face hidden behind a dark, curly beard, wavy hair extending past his ears. All of his features were exaggerated, including his voice, which could have projected across the entire gauntlet. None of the students in the class even reached the height of his shoulders. He had an incredibly intimidating demeanor due to his sheer size, which kept us sapients in line since Professor Ocumulus was the head of Shadow Peaks Hall.

There were no chairs in the laboratory, so we all congregated in one corner of the room.

Four TAs worked the computer stations on the opposite side.

Next to the computers extended a long hallway lined with the simulation pods, one for each student in the class. Each pod was a white dome structure with cables and multi-colored wires snaking along the ceiling and reaching down to the nexus point of each pod, then stretching down each egg-shaped structure like a network of veins.

"Did you all enjoy your time off?" Professor Ocumulus asked, this time seemingly expecting a response.

A handful of nods and unenthusiastic *yeses* ensued.

However, he waited for a more energetic response which didn't appear to be coming.

"Well, I guess we'll jump right into business," he said after more awkward silence. "As I mentioned before the break, the initial machine learning time is done, so the true practice and training can begin. You've already had many hours of experience in the Combative Casting simulator in *training mode*. Today will be your first experience in *combat mode*. The objectives are the same—practicing your budding powers to increase efficiency and effectiveness in stressful situations. Now, we're simply going to increase the stress in a controlled, non-lethal environment. Turn it up to eleven, if you will." He stopped as if waiting for a reaction.

The TAs produced a pitiful display of canned laughter.

The rest of us didn't understand what was supposed to be so funny.

"Never mind," Professor Ocumulus continued. "The assignment is for you to push yourselves. But if at any time the experience becomes too overwhelming, all you have to say is *safe house*, and you will be immediately transported back to the starting point. And when that happens, we'll be alerted of your return, and one of the SEs or I will be quick to check on you."

I'd forgotten that Professor Ocumulus liked to call his TAs simulation engineers—or SEs.

"So, what's the safe word?" he asked.

"*Safe house*," several of us replied.

"It's two words," Erik said, under his breath.

"What was that, Mr. Connelly?" the professor asked.

"*Safe house*," Erik said, pretending he'd said it all along.

"That's what I thought you said." The professor nodded to his engineers, then turned his attention back to us. "Let's not keep talking about the simulation. It's time to experience it. You know where to go. Line up at your assigned pods."

"Is it true the simulation will now include vampires?" a student close to Nym asked.

"Oh, yes. I remembered in the previous classes, which I assume is how you heard about it. Yes, vampires have been added back into the simulation, as approved by the headmistress. It is time to face and conquer the trauma created from last year's tragic events. Continuing to shelter you would be a disservice. Thank you for reminding me. Now you are prepared. Go. Line up."

When no one immediately moved, I gave a solemn look to my friends and marched toward the pods. Nym followed, which motivated Razielle and Erik to continue after us.

As I reached the door to my pod, I realized we'd provided the catalyst for the rest of the class. We were all lined up, yet far from ready. Razielle stood to my right, and Nym to my left. Erik waited a few pods away.

Each pod had a small locker atop a metal post, similar to a mailbox.

There was a hook on one side to hang my backpack, and I placed my valuables inside the locker, including my soul crystal. Crystals were prohibited inside the pods, which typically wasn't an issue since sapients didn't have crystals yet. As usual, I was the exception.

I was also the first seamstress to go through these

simulations, which required some discussions with Headmistress Christi. Special parameters had to be set for my pod since I'd be inside with a needle. There was no way in hell I was removing it every day.

With a swoosh of released air, the pod doors slid open. Everything we'd ever imagined in some form or another awaited us inside those white walls.

The question was, which imaginings would become real today?

CHAPTER 5

I led the class to the pods, and I led the class to enter them. The anticipation was only making my anxious mind worse. For as long as I could remember, I had been the girl who jumped headfirst into messed-up situations, often to my own detriment. But this was one instance where my bad habit was an advantage. This wasn't like jumping out the window of the lonely tower. Nothing inside this pod was literally going to kill me. This was a controlled environment despite what would soon appear. Those words were easy to say while the walls were still white. They were much harder to remember once the walls disappeared and my imagination came to life.

Before the safe house appeared, the inside of the pod was pure white. Once the door slid shut, it fully vanished into the curved wall. It wasn't even noticeable where the walls ended, and the floor began. The whole place was as much of a void as I could imagine —except this void was white compared to the blackness inside an open seam.

The pod was also as devoid of sound as of color.

It was soundproofed to the outside lab.

And the silence only accentuated the ringing in my ears.

I'd always found the transition from white void to safe house jarring, so I closed my eyes before it happened—before the imaginary world appeared.

The start of the simulation would be picked up by my other senses.

The safe house had been designed as a one-room cabin and smelled distinctly of pine, which had become a calming scent. Rustic furniture was sparsely arranged. Several windows showcased the mountain wilderness outside. And when I appeared in the house—or the house appeared around me—I was centered in the room with a thick, circular rug beneath my feet.

I felt the cabin coming into existence, at which time I opened my eyes.

I was standing dead center on the circular rug. The fresh scent of pine wafted into my nostrils. And I could hear the chirping of birds outside.

Everything was as I'd remembered it. I was alone, as was customary—or part of the program. No one else was allowed in my cabin—my *safe house*.

But according to Professor Ocumulus, I now had the ability to say the words and be transported right back here. That had never been a feature before, not that I'd ever previously found myself in a situation where I needed it.

I'd been in several life-and-death encounters up to this point, and never had the luxury of a safe word to conveniently whisk me away to safety.

Well, that may not exactly have been true. My ability to teleport could serve a similar function. It had certainly saved my life on more than a few occasions, even when I hadn't intended it to.

I'm not running from an imaginary foe. I was putting my foot down—setting my intention—before stepping off this rug and exiting the safety of the cabin.

Outside the windows looked as it always did.

A sunny winter's day with snow in the distance. But the view from the windows was as much an illusion as everything else in the simulation. What I saw outside through the windows was not necessarily what I'd find when I walked through the door. Sometimes, I stepped outside, and sometimes, stepped into another room. And once I left the familiarity of the cabin, it was gone.

I emerged onto a town street I'd pictured countless times when younger.

It might have been based off a real street that my subconscious mind remembered from my childhood, or could have been a complete figment of my imagination.

But if it was real, then I hadn't stumbled upon it since Mom had repurchased our old family home in Southern California.

As soon as I touched down onto the sidewalk, I knew why I was here.

I only had one recurring dream taking place on this street. The simulator had never led me here before. I immediately wanted to retreat, but the cabin was gone.

Safe house.

Thinking the words didn't transport me back, and I was tempted to say them aloud.

If this was how the new combat-level simulations would work, then maybe it was worth not venturing any farther into the depths of my demented mind.

I imagined it being early afternoon, not too long after lunch.

The boutiques lining the streets were frequented by window shoppers. Cars passed at a leisurely pace. People needing to be at work already were, so those left had nowhere pressing to be. And I was seemingly one of those people.

I'd never been in the dream before, just always imagining this had been what the street looked like. Now I was on it—an actual observer instead of an omnipresent one.

And just like clockwork, my parents exited one

of the shops ahead of me, holding hands and carrying bags. They were laughing and carefree as they strode down the sidewalk in the same direction as me, swinging their linked arms as they went.

Mom looked like her old self, the way she'd looked when I'd first seen her in Ogginosh.

The way she looked when she'd dropped me off at school that seemingly ordinary morning.

"Mom! Dad!" I called after them, but they didn't hear me. Perhaps they did but didn't suspect they were the ones being addressed. "Tamara! Peter!" The result was no different. I was merely the observer. However, others I passed clearly noticed me. So, I wasn't a ghost after all.

My parents turned into an alley, which led to a backlot where their car was parked. I picked up my pace as they disappeared from view.

I know this isn't real, I reminded myself. *It's only a simulation. It's only created what I gave the machine.* But it appeared so damn real.

My heartrate spiked. A sudden heaviness in my chest almost prevented me from taking in a single breath. Dizziness overwhelmed me. But regardless of how faint I was steadily becoming, I broke into a labored run, desperate to reach them before anything bad happened. I had the abilities to protect them. I was a seamstress with incredible power, and they were just regular people.

The internal story had changed over the years. It

wasn't until recently that I'd discovered my abilities. For most of my life, real magic had not been in the equation.

I rounded the corner still unable to breathe, reaching out to the edge of the storefront to keep myself vertical.

Immediately, I heard the first gunshot, its thunderous sound rooting me to the spot at the entrance of the alley, sending a violent tremor rippling throughout my body. I couldn't even release a scream as my father dropped to the ground. But my mother's cry of anguish somehow dwarfed the thunder of the gunshot, eclipsing the second pull of the trigger.

She folded forward and crumpled to the ground on top of my father.

Blood spilled onto the cracked payment.

I still couldn't move. The ragged man who'd attacked them knelt beside the bodies and rummaged through their pockets. He looked inside the bags they'd been carrying but decided the contents weren't worth stealing. Then he grabbed my mother's purse, straightened up again, stuffed the pistol into the front of his ripped jeans, and ran toward me.

I'd spent the better part of my teenage years fighting anyone who'd got in my way.

I'd attacked Kicryrian soldiers, and I'd slain vampires.

But I couldn't make a single move against the man running toward me. I felt as though I was in first grade again, powerless to protect anyone, including myself.

I wasn't invisible to him, either. He saw me as he frantically approached, our eyes meeting for a fraction of a second. Then he turned onto the sidewalk and escaped into the big, wide world.

No one else seemed to notice anything had happened. Others passed by on the sidewalk, oblivious to the deaths in the alley, talking on their phones or focused straight ahead.

I found my voice and let out a scream, startling a few passersby. But no one stopped.

With my anguished release, I was suddenly freed from my spot at the entrance of the alley. I staggered forward. The awkward pile of limbs and clothes was the first thing that didn't look real.

Blood continued to spread as if bubbling up from the ground. And as I drew closer, I could no longer avoid it. I waded through the congealing pond, not knowing what to do. Still, no one was stopping. I had no phone to call for help. And there was a quiet voice in the back of my mind reminding me there was no one to call. This wasn't real.

However, the voice was quickly drowned out by my own crying.

I splashed onto my knees and dropped my head

to my mother's back, the sobs racking my entire body in rib-crushing fits.

I hadn't been able to save them when I was younger, and wasn't able to save them now. But this was how I'd envisioned the situation unfolding once I'd been told they'd been killed in a mugging gone horribly wrong. The mind filled in the blanks with terrible detail. But even my childhood imagination hadn't been capable of capturing this level of vivid imagery.

"Help!" I cried into my mother's blouse. The word was loud in my head, but I doubted people on the sidewalk could hear me. However, it didn't matter. The small part of me still tethered to the real world knew no such help was coming. My parents weren't even dead. This wasn't real.

But I continued to cry for help with the desperation of someone lost in a dream.

At some point, the scene would disappear, and I'd be back inside the pod. All I could do was wait for that to happen, incapable of doing anything else.

Until I heard a distinct click behind me.

I lifted my head and gazed back with blurry vision, but even through the tears, could make out the silhouette of the man who'd gunned down my parents.

He stood several feet away. His white sneakers had splashes of my parents' blood as he stood in the pool that never seemed to stop expanding. Soon, it would reach the sidewalk, spill into the street, and pour into the gutter like a waterfall.

He'd returned, and the barrel of his gun was now aimed at me. "Give me your wallet," he demanded, gesturing with his empty hand.

"I don't have one on me," I answered, the words uneven as I fought to get them out between sobs. "I don't have anything."

However, the man repeated himself. "Give me your wallet." The words, tone, and inflections didn't change, making him sound like a broken record.

"I can't," I whispered, unable to say anything more.

The broken record repeated, same as before. He wasn't going to leave or take no for an answer. His mission was to engage. I'd experienced interactions like this in the simulation before. The program was pushing me in a certain direction. I was supposed to fight.

It may have been the first time in my life that the fight wasn't in me. I'd been broken into way too many goddamn pieces to pick myself off the ground. Even though I looked nineteen, I felt seven. There was nothing I could do. My seven-year-old self couldn't stop crying. She couldn't handle what was happening. She couldn't fight back. She couldn't…

"Don't make me put a bullet in you like I did to these two," the man said, more determined to encourage me to engage. "Give me your wallet."

"Do what you must," I said, blinking through the tears. As my vision cleared, then so did the silhouette. He was no longer the man I'd pictured before, but another man from my nightmares.

When he demanded my wallet again, his lips didn't move. Red thread crisscrossed his mouth. His grating voice echoed in my head. His bald head glistened in the sunlight. I glimpsed the long legs of the spider tattoo behind his ear.

His beard was long and straggly, smaller black spiders scurrying through the matted hair.

"Have you ever seen arms ripped from a body?" Tarquin asked, still pointing the gun at me.

Bile rose in my throat at the thought of such an act. I immediately pictured the angels with their wings torn from their backs, then thrown from the window of the lonely tower. The screams that followed were just as loud as the voice currently occupying my head.

"You will cut me free, then I'll make you fly."

I scooted away from the heap that had once been my parents, slipping as I moved through the blood. My heart pounded like a jackhammer. At least I was moving.

I wouldn't allow this monster to lay his hands on me.

"You thought I was dead," Tarquin said, his bound lips curling up into a fiendish grin. "But I'm not. You can't—you can't kill me. I'll always come back for you. Your whole family is mine. I will kill you all over and over again. There is no escape."

He kept pace with me as I continued to retreat. His gun was now down by his side. His boots stomping through the thick blood made a sucking sound. A spider descended from a red strand connected to the bottom of his beard.

The thought of those spiders scampering after me through the blood-soaked groundcover was as terrifying as Tarquin himself.

"You're not real," I said, my voice catching on the sickness in the back of my throat. "You're not really here."

"Oh, that's where you're wrong, little bird. I'm very real. And it's just you and me."

I raised a bloody hand, mustering enough concentration to fire an energy ball at him—but it went right through his body as if he was a ghost. Which he was.

A ghost. A ghost I carried with me everywhere.

I made several more shots as he continued to advance, gaining on me as I scrambled backwards on one hand at a time. But none of my shots hit the target. In my desperation, one hand connected awkwardly with the ground and my arm folded, sending me onto my back and splashing into the blood. Luckily, I was able to keep my head high enough not to bounce off the concrete, but it was a miniscule victory.

Tarquin was standing over me the next second. One hand was holding the gun and the other now glowed bright orange. Instead of using the gun, he extended the glowing hand to release a fireball on me just as he had in Ogginosh.

The flaming projectile set me ablaze upon impact, and I was consumed with a familiar agony I never wanted to feel again.

He stood and watched as I screamed, frantically rolling in the blood to suffocate the flames, but they would not yield. Instead, they seemed to grow and spread until I was leaving a trail of flames, moving through the crimson pond.

Tarquin stepped back as the flames neared him.

The flickering orange demon reached toward my parents, and soon they were engulfed as well. Soon, we'd all be ashes in the remote alley, gone from this world forever.

The pain was so blinding, everything stopped functioning. My rolling stopped. My movements stopped. My screaming stopped. My vision beyond the flames faded from view, including my parents— including Tarquin. I could no longer remember how I'd gotten here. My parents' random murder made no sense. Tarquin arriving out of nowhere made no sense. Me being back in Southern California made no sense. I couldn't understand what was happening because the only thing holding my focus was the heat of the flames and the pain of my body melting away.

I was supposed to remember something about a house, but it was like grasping for another ghost. I was forgetting something important, something bound to be lost forever. The pain wouldn't allow me to concentrate on anything else. So, there was nothing left I could do.

Why is this happening to me?

All I could hope for was to black out and allow all of this to end. And it wasn't long before I got my wish…

Except everything didn't turn black, but white.

The flames were instantly gone. The blood beneath me was gone. The entire world I'd been existing in was gone.

The pain didn't instantly dissolve with the scenery, but steadily dissipated as my mind caught up to what was happening.

I was waking from an elaborate dream—a virtual-reality simulation tailored specifically for me. I had done this many times, but it had never felt like this. I had never been so consumed by the dream that I'd completely forgotten what reality was.

It took me several moments of lying on the floor and looking up at the white dome ceiling of the pod to remember where I was. What day it was.

Hell, what year it was.

My parents are alive. Tarquin is dead. It was only a simulation. Nothing I saw or experienced was real.

I squeezed my eyes shut as I let all the air out of my lungs. My exhaustion was real. My inability to stand was real. And the tears now flowing down the sides of my cheeks were also very goddamn real.

CHAPTER 6

No one wanted to talk about what they'd experienced in Combative Casting. Obviously, I wasn't the only one with a traumatic encounter. I was willing to talk about almost anything, but my time in the pod was just too raw. And since the rest of my friends were keeping their experiences to themselves, I wasn't going to be the only one to share.

Dinner was less lively than lunch.

I still wasn't hungry, even though I'd thrown out a good part of my lunch.

It was always hard to tell what Nym was thinking these days, so her introspection was nothing new. Razielle was typically an open book, but she'd been uncommonly quiet since we'd left class.

Like me, the problem with my roommates was

that we'd seen and experienced more than most. And those experiences drove the simulation.

I wondered how many previous students completely cracked from the simulations. It seemed inevitable. What was the percentage? How many of us would succumb to a similar fate?

"I know you both don't want to talk about it," I said once we got back to our room after the somber dinner. "I don't, either. But are you both okay? Will you be?"

"I don't even know how to answer that question," Razielle said, climbing to the top bunk and crashing to the mattress. In doing so, she disappeared and made no attempt to look over the edge.

"We have to sit through other classes tomorrow. How am I supposed to concentrate in other classes when I'm just thinking about having to go back in there? Then we have to do it all over again." She paused. "I can't handle it again."

"Yes, you can," I assured her. "We all can. We may not want to repeat the experience, but we can handle it. And besides, how many of your earlier simulations repeated themselves?"

"I know that's supposed to make me feel better, but it just means they will get worse. We don't have to worry about the awful event being repeated, but some new event even more awful than the last."

"I don't know what's coming next, but it's not necessarily worse. Or maybe the same simulation won't be so bad the second time. You'll know what's coming. You'll know how to handle it better. You'll know what to do."

"I couldn't remember the safe word," Nym said, huddled up on her bed. "I couldn't get out. I was locked in there until the professor called time. I don't want that to happen again."

"Me neither," Razielle said. "If I could, I would have used it. And it was so freakin' simple. But I couldn't remember it!"

It made me feel better to know I wasn't the only one. I felt crazy for forgetting it myself, assuming I was the only one. But I hadn't been. We'd all been trapped in our own personal Hells.

"If it's any consolation, I bet we had it worse than the others," I said. "Worse than the rest of the group —worse than the rest of the classes. And it makes us the strongest of the bunch."

"I don't feel very strong right now," Nym said. "I felt stronger as a plain ol' half elf."

"We'll do better tomorrow." I rapped on the underside of the top bunk. "You hear me up there? We'll do better tomorrow."

"Yeah, I hear you," Razielle groaned. "I have a hard time believing you, but I hear you."

"One thing I think might help is to go back in there remembering we're not fighting alone. We may be fighting separately, but we're not fighting alone."

"Separate by definition means *not together* or *alone*."

"When we were fighting in the Battle of Spell-crest—either one—we weren't fighting the same opponents. We were both fighting—separate, but not alone."

"I'll try it tomorrow," Nym said. "Though it may be harder for me than the rest of you."

"Why's that?" I asked.

Nym simply shook her head. "I can't. But I'll try to remember what you said despite who I have to fight in there."

"And my thoughts will be with you too."

"My thoughts will be with trying to remember the damn safe word. *Safe house*," Razielle said with a sigh. "It doesn't get any easier than that."

"I know," I said, then perked up to a knock at the door.

"Go away!" Razielle yelled. "I'm not in the mood for company!"

"Did you ever think it might not be for you?" I said, hopping off the bed to answer the door.

I was greeted with a sympathetic smile, and did the best I could to return the smile before Devon folded me into his strong arms.

"Tough day?" he asked, resting his hand at the base of my neck.

"You could say that," I said.

"First day of the second trimester of your sapient

year. I remember it well. In fact, I can still feel it. It's a shock that hopefully won't be rivaled."

"Are you trying to tell us it'll get better?"

"It does."

"What sadist came up with this stupid simulation?" Razielle said, now peeking her head over the wooden railing of her top bunk.

"Professor Ocumulus did," Devon said. "He developed and perfected it with his brother."

"That crazy looking brute has a brother?"

"I don't know anything about him other than him also being a professor here years ago—before my time."

"Where's he now?" Nym asked.

Devon kissed my cheek, continuing farther into the room. "Dead. I remember hearing about him when I was a sapient and another student asking him the same question. That was all he said. And no one dared ask a follow-up question."

"Maybe his simulation killed him," Razielle said sarcastically, then dropped back out of view.

"Has anyone died from the simulation?" Nym asked.

Devon tensed, providing the dreaded answer without saying a word.

"Then why is it still part of the curriculum?" I asked.

"You don't want to hear about this right now," Devon said.

"Are you kidding?" Razielle scoffed, reappearing at the edge of the bunk. "We freakin' need to hear it now!"

"I have to agree with Razielle," I said. "What's the story?"

"Only what I heard when I was a sapient," Devon said. "And it was the first or second year of the simulation, which was like thirty years ago. There was a student with some special medical condition and his body shut down right in the middle of the simulation. It didn't have the number of sensors it does now, so no one noticed until the end of class. By that time, there was nothing they could do to revive him. He was already gone. It's been upgraded many times since then. A lot safer now. I know it's intense, but you have nothing to worry about. If your vitals approach a dangerous zone, the simulation will shut down, notifying Professor Ocumulus immediately."

"That makes me feel *so* much better," Razielle sighed, and again rolled out of view.

"No one's died since?" I asked.

"Not that I'm aware of," Devon said. He tried to pull me into a hug, but I kept him at bay while considering his answer. "I mean, there have been incidents of the simulation being shut down because of a student being overwhelmed. But the professor helped them, and they fully recovered, which shows the emergency protocols are working."

"The need for emergency protocols shows there's a problem," Nym said.

"You're not going up against live enemies, which would be much more dangerous. This is what the Academy came up with to provide you with a life-like experience at a fraction of the risk." Devon paused while we all considered what he'd said. "I know it's hard. It's supposed to be hard. But like I said, it *will* get better."

"I want to believe you," Nym said, hugging her legs even tighter than before.

"I'm ready to be a Master Classman already," Razielle said, her voice floating from overhead.

"Once you get past this, then you will be," Devon said. His gaze was trained on me as he spoke.

I needed to get fresh air, and it was clear the girls wanted their space. We all needed time to decompress. Not too long ago, I would have wanted to do that work on my own, but now I wanted Devon with me. He helped calm me. It wasn't like our tumultuous beginning anymore, though it helped we were on a level playing field—each with a needle of our own.

"I'm glad you called," Devon said as we made our way down the stairs, headed out into the brisk evening air. "I knew today would be tough, but didn't want to impose."

"You're never an imposition," I said.

There were fewer students out around Shadow

Peaks Hall, but as we neared the cafeteria and the other dormitories, it started feeling more normal. I thought it would be best to get away from Spellcrest for a little while, so we ventured into the village.

I grabbed a root beer from one of the markets, though Devon opted for a plain ol' water.

Many of the tables arranged around the square were empty, so we had our pick. I leaned back in my chair with my leather jacket unzipped—the octagram tattoo and soul crystal at my chest keeping me warm—and sipped my root beer.

"I remember this day," Devon said, sitting across from me, both elbows propped on the metal table. "The first day of the second trimester of my sapient year. Three years ago. It doesn't feel that long ago. Very few of us weren't impacted by this day. It's a memory that sticks with you and provides context for everything to come.

"I'm not going to say it gets easier. It doesn't. But you become stronger. Better able to handle whatever's thrown at you because you're conquering the things you don't want others to even know about you. It's not like just fighting some bullies pushing you around on campus. The simulation is shown your true demons and exposes them for you to strike down.

"I couldn't talk about my experience with anyone because my true identity was hidden from my friends. Even my girlfriend at the time didn't know."

"That's right—the girl who broke up with you when she graduated?" I said.

"Yeah. Clara. She knows now, but didn't at the time, so I went through this experience alone. It was tough. It wasn't like my mother had much sympathy."

"She's not exactly the mothering type, though she's less intense since she returned—I'll give her that."

"She *has* changed. I guess death has a way of changing people—even the hard cases like my mother," Devon said, allowing a low chuckle. "I had to go through it alone. But you don't have anything to hide from your friends, or from me. Not like I did. I envisioned my father on that first simulation. I hadn't been there when he was killed, but pictured what it must have been like a million times. And I vowed to kill the man who murdered him. Of course, I was young when it happened and there was nothing I could really do about it—but I wanted vengeance, nevertheless.

"I had no picture of the man who did it until years later, but I created a vivid image in my mind— one of a shadowed man who haunted me for years."

"Didn't you tell me that Tarquin killed your father?" I asked, trying to remember the context of the conversation. Then I was reminded of a moment we shared under the bleachers of Hollywood High, after he'd been thrown from the window of the lonely tower, and I'd jumped out after him.

"Tarquin Drome," Devon said with the utmost disdain, as if the name was physically painful to say. "It was hard to believe I could create a more sinister vision than the man who'd done the deed, but somehow I'd managed it. He was there, but so was the real man. By that time, I'd been shown a picture of the real Tarquin. Mouth sewn shut and all. And I was forced to battle them both... after watching my father get struck down just like he'd been so many times in my head. I won't go into the gory detail, but you get the gist of it."

I did. All too well. My heart went out to him, hearing the pain in his voice. And I knew exactly how he must be feeling... because I'd endured the same scenario.

I couldn't believe how our simulations seemed to mirror one another.

Or maybe the simulation had picked up on us being damaged in the same ways, requiring the same protocols to overcome them.

Then the heartbreaking difference hit me.

I'd gotten *my* parents back. Devon's father had never returned.

"I'm sorry, Devon," I said, working hard to keep my composure. "These past few years, I've been so focused on the Tarquin of my nightmares, I was blinded to the fact he was just as much your boogeyman." I cupped a hand around the crystal as it started to glow, as if Tarquin knew we were talking about him.

"It's okay. That's what I'm getting at." Devon produced a sad smile. "You needed to kill him. You needed the vengeance. By that time, I'd killed him a hundred times, gotten my revenge, even if it was only a simulation. It was real enough to me."

"Wow…" was all I could say.

"Like I said, I know it's hard," he reiterated. "And it's not going to get easier. But what each session means to you will change, as will you. And one day, the angry hole you can never seem to fill won't be so deep anymore. Then the true healing can begin." Devon took a deep breath. "I never told the story of my first unlocked simulation to anyone before. It's freeing. If you don't want to talk about your experience with me, then I suggest you tell your roommates."

"If I told you now, you'd just think I was copying you," I said, producing a guilty smile, then taking another sip of my sweet soda.

"You watched your parents die too?"

I nodded. "And Tarquin was right there to torment me. However, I wasn't strong enough to kill him. He essentially killed me, then I woke up back in the pod."

"I didn't kill him the first time either," Devon said. "I reached the point of being able to kill him—

then I did it many times. But I couldn't do it in the early days." He paused and glanced around before continuing. "Do you want to know a secret?"

"*Always*," I said, leaning into the table.

"As you might know, one of the privileges of being the headmistress's son is overhearing a few things students aren't supposed to know. So, I'll ask you not to spread this around. But no one kills their demon in the first fight. *No one*. It's not that everyone's weak, but the simulation won't allow it. It's programmed to ensure you're bested."

"What? Why?"

"The conquering of your demon—or demons—must be a journey. You must grow, advance, improve in order to succeed. It's how the simulation is designed."

"So, we were all beaten down today, so we can be built back up?" I asked.

"Exactly," Devon said. "I know you have more demons than most, and you're not at the same level as the others. So, I don't feel bad about you having this information. And I can already tell, despite how hard you thought today was, you're already moving past it."

"I try not to dwell."

"I remember." Devon offered a smile, which grew as he seemingly pictured a fond memory.

As I took another sip of my root beer, I gazed out at the mostly empty square. Many of the shops were getting ready to close for the night. Patrons were heading home. A few couples or families occupied other tables, but most of them were empty.

Then my eyes stopped on one occupied table with a single man sitting at it, bundled up in a black winter coat. His face was shrouded in shadows, but he was positioned in our direction.

There was no food arranged in front of him. I couldn't see his eyes, but if I didn't know any better, I'd swear he was staring at us.

"There's a creepy guy behind you watching us," I said, turning my attention to Devon.

"Oh yeah?" he said and immediately turned in his chair. "Where?"

When my gaze relocated the table, I discovered it was no longer occupied.

I glanced around, searching for the man walking away, but didn't see him anywhere. As suddenly as I'd noticed him from across the village square, he'd disappeared.

CHAPTER 7

"*I*t's time to go," I said to Razielle, still refusing to get out of bed. Now she was on the top bunk, she was harder to reach—unless I climbed up there.

"You said that already," Razielle whined.

"And yet you're still not moving. Get the hell up!"

"I'm up."

Nym was giving herself a final check in the mirror on her wardrobe door, then grabbed her backpack, and was ready to go. She didn't have Divination with Razielle and me, but we were all headed to the Manor.

"If you're going to make me late, then I'm leaving ahead of you girls," Nym threatened.

"I said I'm up." Razielle groggily climbed down the bunk ladder and opened her wardrobe.

"Hurry up and change," I said.

"Screw it. I'm going like this." Razielle threw a coat on over her pajamas and grabbed a pair of boots. "It's not my fault I didn't get any sleep last night. I don't know how the both of you are so chipper and productive this morning."

"I wouldn't say I'm either of those things," I said.

"I didn't sleep well either," Nym said.

"But don't vampires need less sleep to function?" Razielle asked.

"I don't know. I'm still tired. I'm just doing what's necessary to get to class on time."

Razielle gave a mocking response as if she was five years old and tucked her flannel pajamas pants into her snow boots. She took a moment to fix her deteriorating bun.

Then she looked spastically around the room for her backpack, apparently forgetting she leaves it propped next to her desk every day.

"There, I'm ready. Happy now?" she said, once her backpack was slung over one shoulder.

"Let's get this day over with," I said, and we all headed out the door.

Even with everything Devon had told me last night, I still dreaded my next visit into the simulation. I was afraid for my friends' mental health even more so than my own.

There was a method to the madness, but it was still madness. I couldn't wait for us to get a week or more under our belts, so our days could return to normal levels of classroom stress. We just came back from vacation, and I already needed another one.

We were running a few minutes late, but plenty of students were still making their way to the Manor. It felt like the type of morning which should have been shadowed by dark clouds, but the sky was bright and blue, the sun now rising over the Academy wall.

"I wish I could get drunk," Razielle said. "Alcohol's supposed to take your mind off things, or so I'm told."

"It's a false promise," I said. "Trust me. You're better off without it."

"Sleeping pills then. Those probably wouldn't work on me, either. I've never tried."

"I'm sure we'll all sleep better tonight. And if you need me to, I can always crack you over the head."

"I don't like the sound of that."

"I'll take my chances with the nightmares," Nym said.

"Good," I said with a chuckle. "Because I didn't want to do it anyway."

Razielle and I said goodbye to Nym once we reached the Manor. I made sure she didn't venture back into Memorial Hall before headed toward our classroom.

Once we entered the classroom, Razielle pointed out the new TA immediately.

"That's gotta be her. Miss Long."

I was impressed that even with how exhausted she was, Razielle still remembered the new TA's name. Ivanic had mentioned it yesterday, but I'd forgotten. It wasn't overly important to me, which wasn't the case with Razielle. Miss Long was unknowingly her new nemesis.

We grabbed two seats near the back, and Razielle continued to stare daggers at the TA while she cheerfully chatted with a nearby student.

Now, I could understand why the boys didn't want to admit whether they thought she was pretty or not. I could objectively say she was freakin' gorgeous.

Her facial features were soft and radiant. Thick and wavy white hair spilled onto her shoulders. Her eyes were kind and nearly looked lavender. I couldn't tell her height since she was sitting, but it was clear she had envious curves.

Razielle and most of the boys in the class were doing enough staring, so I tried not to add to the attention aimed at her.

I still believed Ivanic would be faithful, but this wolf shifter TA certainly was going to throw a wrench in their relationship—knowingly or not.

Razielle leaned across the aisle. "She's kind of ugly. I *so* don't have anything to worry about."

"*Totally*," I answered, trying to be as supportive as humanly possible, even though it was hard.

Professor Lin swept into the classroom, looking disheveled and sleep-deprived herself.

She dropped her shoulder bag and a few books onto her desk, greeted Miss Long, and quickly quieted the class.

"Today, we will continue our exploration of the divination discipline of Astragalomancy," Professor Lin said and emptied her small leather bag of vertebrae. She'd painted red numbers on each of the bones, which had come from a racoon.

She read off numbers from the scattered bones on her display desk, and Miss Long wrote them on the whiteboard.

"Miss Long, what do you see from the arrangement of numbers?" the professor asked.

"You will receive an unexpected visitor soon," Miss Long said. "Before the third quarter moon."

"Which is when?"

"Umm… Friday, I think."

"Very good. That's what I read as well. And it should be a positive thing with the seven starting off the sequence. So, I'm excited to discover who my unexpected visitor is."

Then she had Miss Long explain how she'd come up with the answer she gave, what the different numbers in the sequence meant.

Getting good at this divination discipline required memorizing because it wasn't about interpreting pictures or designs, but sequencing strings of numbers which appeared random. To the masters of this discipline, the numbers told a story—a story the rest of us couldn't see.

Professor Lin spent half the class going through more history of Astragalomancy, then half the students got a chance to scatter the bones.

Razielle and I were both in the group to receive readings today.

Sarah would get her chance tomorrow.

When it was Razielle's turn, she held the leather bag for a long time before spilling the bones onto the table. There was a point at which I thought she might hand the filled bag back to the professor and decline the reading altogether. Once the professor started reading the numbers, Razielle looked as though she was waiting for the results of a midterm she hadn't studied for.

Not expecting great news but hoping for the best.

I had my fingers crossed for her as well, given everything I knew she was worried about.

"Miss Long, what do you see?" the professor asked.

"You will lose something close to you within the next moon cycle," she said, glancing nervously at Razielle.

"Something or someone?" Razielle asked, posing her question to Professor Lin.

"It's possible to interpret it either way, but I believe it to be *something* as well."

"I don't like the sound of that."

"Remember, the numbers work in mysterious ways—the ways of the universe. Much of it beyond our comprehension. We can make educated guesses, but we're not provided an exact roadmap. We can be guided, but there is still much that remains unseen, which will continue to alter our destinies. Do not fret too much. I'm sure it's nothing life-shattering."

Professor Lin offered a conciliatory smile.

"Go, Maeve," Razielle said, stepping away from the table. "Hopefully, you have better luck than me."

"I don't want to go after that," I said, but the professor waved me over and handed me the refilled bag.

I took a deep breath and closed my eyes as I let the bones fall. When I opened them, the professor was holding one of the bones in her hand.

"It's best to keep your eyes open as you roll. This one fell off the table. Put them back in the bag and reroll."

"Great, this is going to change my whole destiny. I can feel it." I emptied the bag and watched as the final bone knocked into several others, causing more than one to alter their positioning—changing their numbers. I cringed as the professor and Miss Long analyzed the arrangement.

Professor Lin looked confused, not reading the numbers right away as she'd done previously. Confused or concerned... But before I could read too much into it, she read the numbers for Miss Long to write onto the board.

Before giving her TA a chance to speak, she interpreted the numbers herself.

"You will be tested before the new moon," Professor Lin said.

Miss Long looked incredulously at her, her mouth opening as if she was about to say something, but a warning glance from the professor kept her from doing so.

"That's pretty vague," I said.

"Sometimes, the numbers aren't as clear as other times. I understand it can apply to a great many things—especially in a school environment. For instance, I understand Combative Casting is very challenging for each of you right now."

"Then we'd all have the same readings."

"It doesn't work like that." But without wanting to discuss it further, the professor gathered up the bones and ushered the next student to approach the table.

Razielle and I headed back to our desks, both of us rather frustrated with our readings.

"You got me up for this?" Razielle complained as she plopped into her chair with a sigh. "I don't need things to get worse."

"Don't read too much into it," I said. "I don't really believe in this stuff anyway. It's like astrology and other predictive disciplines. It's vague on purpose because it's not really telling you anything unique. Whatever is said can fit into your life one way or another. It feels like magic, but that's after stretching to make a connection."

"Maybe that's part of your test… turning you from a non-believer into a believer. I guess we'll find out soon enough. Let's see what the hell I'm going to lose. And if it's Ivanic, I swear I'm gonna kill that bitch."

Her intensity made me laugh, which I had to quickly stifle to keep from pissing her off more. She was serious. Her death glare was for real. Hopefully, it wouldn't come to violence. Maybe keeping Razielle from killing Miss Long would be my test—if I believed in this divination stuff.

CHAPTER 8

I *will be tested before the new moon.*
Even though they didn't really mean anything, the words stuck with me throughout the morning. This was why I hated Divination. It made these cryptic predictions that could be interpreted any way you like, yet still made you paranoid.

A part of me had to believe in it because otherwise, I wouldn't be stressing about it.

All the other magic I'd learned so far had been real, so why would Divination be the one exception? This thought got under my skin, making me itch.

And then there was the prediction Razielle was dealing with. I would be tested, but she would lose something dear to her. We both knew what she thought it might be, which was something I simply couldn't accept. Ivanic was crazy about her. Even the

MICHAEL PIERCE

wolfish, womanly wiles of Miss Long couldn't get in the way of their storybook relationship.

However, I'd been yet to convince Razielle of this.

Professor Haricot wasn't thrilled with my lack of enthusiasm in Multi-World History, but my mind was plagued with too many other things. Luckily, such lack of enthusiasm was nearly expected in Non-Magical Studies, so I could let my mind wander at will.

Not only was I plagued with the earlier predictions, but I was also haunted by the simulation, which I drew nearer to reentering with each passing period. My time with Devon was helpful, and I'd at least been able to get minimal sleep to function, but I still had an abundance of reservations.

Once I made it to Advanced Evocation, I realized I wasn't the only one. Bree and Ivanic had just come from Combative Casting, and they looked loads worse than yesterday.

"What happened?" I asked Bree as she plopped into her chair.

She dropped her head onto the table in the same breath.

"What didn't happen?" she said, shielding her face in her arms. "I think I need to go back to my room."

"Apparently, her pod wasn't in combat mode yesterday," Ivanic said from the table behind. "So, she

84

wasn't subjected to the true horror the rest of us were until today."

"I feel sick," Bree said. "I shouldn't have come here."

"She fainted after stepping out of the pod."

"Oh my God, Bree. I'm so sorry," I said, gently reaching a hand over to stroke her hair. "Did you hurt yourself?"

"I don't really know how to answer…"

"She was able to make it to a seated position before passing out," Ivanic said. "So at least she didn't fully keel over."

"And how are you?" I asked, glancing back at the fearless cougar. Seated beside him, Erik, looked as if he'd been about to ask the same question.

"I've been better," Ivanic said, trying to sound casual, but he wasn't that good a liar. This was a good thing for Razielle.

"You didn't seem that bad yesterday," Erik said.

"Maybe I was still in shock. Maybe it hadn't fully hit me yet," Ivanic said.

"But it hit you today," I said.

Ivanic nodded. "Not just for myself, but how much everyone else is affected. The haunted faces of the other students. Bree collapsing to the floor. Another girl fainted as well. She'd barely made it out of her pod."

"Good morning, class," Professor Quail said, clapping his hands to get everyone's attention. "I understand this is a difficult time of year, but classes must go on. I assure you, you'll get through this. Sapients do every year."

We were instructed to repeat the exercise from yesterday—of reaching into our partner's mind and extracting the dominant word.

The excitement from yesterday was nonexistent. I tried to encourage Bree, but it was a hopeless cause. And besides her moping and moaning, I had my own shit to deal with. There certainly weren't any successes in our group today. Luckily, today's test wasn't graded.

After Advanced Evocation, we lost Bree for lunch. As the remaining three of us walked to the cafeteria, Erik got a call from Sarah, who'd just gotten out of Combative Casting.

She wanted him to console her.

"And then there were two," Ivanic said once Erik sped away in the direction of Shadow Peaks Hall.

"Are you gonna ditch me too?" I asked, offering a sad smile.

"How is Raz handling all this?"

"About as well as the rest of us, I'd imagine. But it's Nym I'm worried about. I don't think her experience in the simulator is like the rest of ours."

"No. Instead of her fighting the bad guys, she *is* the bad guy. That can't be easy, especially for someone like her."

"She's not now and will never be a bad guy," I said.

"I know," Ivanic seconded. "But I don't know if she knows it anymore."

"Then it's our job to make sure she does."

Razielle and Nym were already in line for food when Ivanic and I entered the bustling cafeteria. We joined our friends, essentially cutting in line, but no one behind us protested. It was hard to tell who the other students were more afraid of now, Nym or me. Probably Nym. And my heart sank at the sad thought.

"I don't see anyone else yet," Razielle said as we started to look for a table.

"No one else is coming," I said. "Bree and Sarah are in bad shape from this morning's simulation, and Erik went to be with his girl."

"I was trying not to think about it. It's probably just as well. I don't want to hear a damn thing about it." Then she eyed Ivanic accusatorily. "You better not say a damn word."

"My lips are sealed," Ivanic promised, without a hint of sarcasm.

Nym looked paler than usual when we sat down to eat, though I didn't know if it was associated with her transition. I sure as hell wasn't going to ask her. Not today.

Beyond our table, the cafeteria seemed less bois-terous, which I was sure had to do with a quarter of the academy population not ecstatically engaged in conversation. The other sapients were easy to pick out, even if I didn't recognize them. Their depressed demeanor gave them away. And our table was no less depressing.

"Ivanic said it wasn't as bad as yesterday," I finally said, getting tired of the silence and picking at my food. "There's hope."

"Bree and Sarah's absence tells me otherwise," Razielle retorted.

"I don't want to go in there again," Nym said. She sounded like her old self, which scared me more than the immortal being she was turning into. She was dreadfully afraid.

I couldn't imagine what she was experiencing in her sadistic, artificial reality.

"It's true," Ivanic said, the only one of us with a semi-normal appetite. "That's what I was telling Maeve on the way over here. Yesterday was *way* worse. Now that the band aid's off, it's not so bad."

Razielle stared at him incredulously. "I don't believe you. And you promised not to say a damn word."

Ivanic went back to his food, not able to hold her gaze. "I was just trying to help."

"We're all tough women here," I proclaimed. "And Ivanic. We survived yesterday and we'll survive again today. We can do this. Magic is all about belief —belief in yourself. Think of how much we've learned over the past few years. We can do this too." When no one commented—*or stopped me*—I kept going. "This isn't the real thing. And we've *battled* the real thing. We know what we're capable of."

"Yeah... I do... and that's what scares me the most," Nym finally said, her words immediately shutting me up.

"I'm sorry, Nym," I said. "But I know we'll get through this. All of us, which includes *you*."

"I know I'll make it through the simulation. That's not really what I'm worried about."

"Then what is it?"

"It's what happens afterward... once I'm no longer in the simulation... I couldn't live with myself if my simulation became a self-fulfilling prophecy."

"What are you having to go through in there?" Ivanic asked.

Nym simply looked at him and shook her head. No one pressed her.

We wasted a lot more food, tossing most of what we'd chosen at the beginning of lunch. We'd been hopeful, but our stomachs had not agreed. Hopeful didn't equate to hungry.

Ivanic gave Razielle a long hug before leaving us girls to our nightmarish fates. He almost looked as if he was going to hug me next, then thought better of it and left before any words of jealousy could rear their ugly head.

CHAPTER 9

I was almost surprised to see Erik when we reached the basement classroom, and he didn't look any better than the rest of us.

"How are Sarah and Bree doing?" I asked.

"Not great," he said, solemnly. "Sarah tried to get me to skip today—and I must say, I nearly did. But I decided I couldn't be the only one in the group copping out."

"I'm glad you're here," Razielle said.

"We all are," I seconded.

"Yeah, well, that makes one of us," Erik said.

As it neared the start time, I surveyed the room and determined quite a few people were missing. We hadn't been the only ones who'd contemplated ditching.

And those of us who'd showed up looked regretful for doing so.

"He hasn't seen us yet," Razielle whispered to the rest of the huddled group. "We can still get out of here."

But before we could come to a consensus, Professor Ocumulus emerged from his office behind the pods, quickly greeted his simulation engineers, then approached the nervously waiting sapients.

"There's always increased absenteeism on the second day of the second trimester, and this year is no exception," he said, his voice as bold as his stature. "Thank you for those of you here, willing to face your fears. That's the only way through. Putting off the inevitable—*procrastinating*—will only prolong conquering those fears. And I can assure you, you *will* conquer them."

"Well, aren't we the lucky ones," Razielle said under her breath.

After Professor Ocumulus reiterated the safe word, we lined up before our dedicated simulation pods.

It was time. *No putting off the inevitable now.*

I placed my valuables in the small locker, including my crystal, then took a string of deep breaths—doing whatever I could to remain calm. My heart was already racing as my fear rose from the desperate thoughts of what awaited me inside that virtual world.

"It's time," the professor said, when no one was stepping into the pods.

I was about to lead the way again when Nym stepped forward before I could. She didn't look at any of us. Our little vampire elf entered her simulation pod first. My first reaction was pride, but it was quickly overshadowed by fear.

You got this, little elf.

I nodded to Razielle and Erik before stepping into my own pod, where I was quickly enveloped by an expanse of white.

I knew the introductory routine. I closed my eyes while waiting for the simulation to activate, not needing my eyes to know when the environment changed. Within seconds, I was standing in the middle of the mountain cabin. It looked so serene and innocent.

I could remain right here—in my safe house. I didn't have to venture outside. No one would come for me here. They couldn't. Otherwise, it wouldn't be a safe house.

This was the first time I'd considered not leaving the cabin, and I didn't know what would happen if I refused to move from the spot to which I was currently rooted.

"If I don't venture out, then I'm no better than the kids who refused to come to class," I said, essentially talking to myself. However, it was evident my conversations in here were being recorded for review and training purposes. At least, I hoped that was the extent to which the recordings were being used.

I thought of how my friends were faring in their own nightmare worlds. Were they all standing in their safe houses, considering whether to open the doors?

The longer I stood there, the harder it was to move—the more I dreaded what would appear on the other side of the exterior door. But the longer I stood rooted to the spot, the more upset I became with myself. It wasn't until my disappointment over-powered my fear that I was able to take those pivotal steps forward. And once I did—once I threw the door open, all my dread was realized.

Instantly, I found myself back on the familiar sidewalk, familiar faces obliviously exiting a small-town boutique, with new purchases swinging from their unlinked hands.

"Mom! Dad!" I yelled, and still, they didn't hear me. I was invisible to them—unable to stop what was about to happen—*again*.

I ran after them, getting to the alley quicker this time, but still not before the first gunshot went off, with all the horror destined to repeat itself. Again, I was forced to watch my parents die. Again, I was forced to confront the gunman. And again, I was attacked by the sewn man of my nightmares—Tarquin Drome.

He was even more unnatural and superhuman

this time, making me feel as if a counterattack would be futile. And again, I froze, unable to fight as I'd done all my life. Once I found myself on fire for the second time in two days, all memory of the simple safe word eluded me.

All I could do was endure the agony until the fabricated world melted away and I was left with the sterile, white pod. It had become a womb. Or a purgatory.

A blank waiting room where I awaited salvation or damnation.

I fought to steady my breathing. I looked myself over to ensure my body was still whole. No blood. No burned flesh. But the memories were seared into my aching brain.

I slowly got to my feet, then stumbled to the pod door on shaking legs.

Day two. Check.

I'd survived, but hadn't succeeded. I didn't want to think about how many times it would take until I did. Devon had said he'd faced his nemesis hundreds of times. And the one who haunted our dreams was the same man—the man imprisoned in the crystal just outside my simulation pod.

My friends looked the way I felt, and the four of us marched out of the room like zombies. The rest of them had time before their concentration classes. I, on the other hand, had a meeting with the head-mistress. My concentration was special, and it was something only the headmistress was equipped to teach. I was a seamstress, and it was time I learned to act like one.

"You're not coming back to the room with us?" Razielle asked as I headed toward the entrance on the main level.

"I can't. Headmistress Christi is expecting me," I said, sourly.

"Are you okay?" Nym asked.

"Okay as any of you. I'll be fine."

My friends gave me somber nods, then we parted ways.

A chill swept through me as I reached the brisk afternoon air. I wasn't one to feel the cold any longer, especially with the warmth of my tattoo and crystal at my chest, but the chill swept through me just the same, as if I'd stepped through a ghost.

Snow covered the grounds and meticulously placed topiaries. The sky was gray, with nowhere for the distant sun to peek through. Shadow Peaks Hall was the closest dormitory to the Manor, which stood tall with its jagged roof against the dreary backdrop. I gazed up at the cylindrical turret that housed the headmistress's magical office, picturing her waiting on the far couch for my arrival.

She'd been far too nice to me this year, since I'd started my official seamstress training. The nicer and more accommodating she was, the more nervous and suspicious I became. The more time I spent with her, the more I felt she was different. A different woman had come back from the other side. Devon couldn't see it because he was too close to her. However, I couldn't explain why my mother didn't notice.

"Maeve!" a female voice called. Frantic footsteps sounded behind me.

I stopped and turned. "Miss Long?"

The TA from Divination was running far too gracefully down the sidewalk, looking anything but frantic. When she reached me, her substantial chest was heaving, which she placed a hand to as she caught her breath.

"I guess I just missed you at Shadow Peaks," she said between slowing breaths. "Your roommates said you were on your way to meet with the headmistress."

"That's right," I said. "I think I'm already running late."

"Then I'll walk with you."

"Sure. I guess." I started walking, and Miss Long took stride beside me. "What's the sudden emergency? Is there some Divination homework I forgot about?"

"No." She almost laughed, but a seriousness to her countenance quickly returned. "Do you promise not to tell Professor Lin that I talked to you?"

I suddenly forgot about walking toward the Manor. "What? Why?"

The stunning she-wolf bore her lavender eyes into mine. "If I'm to tell you what I came here to tell you, then I need you to promise me."

She looked dead serious, and I thought back to the cryptic message I received in Divination, wondering if that was the reason she was here. I recalled a strange non-verbal exchange between Miss Long and Professor Lin while interpreting my numbers.

"Sure. I promise not to say a word," I said, which seemed to visibly calm her intensity. "What's going on?"

"Do you remember your reading from this morning?"

"Of course. *How could I forget?*" I rolled my eyes. "I will be tested before the new moon. It's not as if I had to wait that long. I just came from Combative Casting and was tested plenty."

"Your reading shouldn't have been expressed as *tested*," Miss Long said.

"Then what should it have—"

"It should have been *attacked*."

I let the word sink in for a moment. She'd said it as if it would be some huge revelation, but I didn't see much of a difference. "I was *attacked* in Combative Casting too," I said. "Same difference."

"As if I could forget, I remember Combative Casting Three as the pod simulations," Miss Long said. "As I said on the first day, I attended Spellcrest too, a few years back. I know you missed it. But the bones do not typically see simulations. They see real life."

"But Professor Lin said—"

"I know what Professor Lin said, which is why I'm here now. She obviously didn't want to scare you. But I see it as a disservice not to tell you the truth.

"Clara?" a familiar voice said, breaking my connection with the Divination TA. "What are you doing here?"

Devon was suddenly standing between us, his face a mask of confusion.

"I'm interning with Professor Lin this trimester," Miss Long—Clara—said.

Why does that name sound familiar?

"And you didn't think to tell me?" Devon asked, almost sounding hurt—or disappointed.

"I didn't want to stir anything up." Her gaze lowered.

"Wait a second," I interjected. "What's going on here?"

"Maeve, this is my ex-girlfriend," Devon said. "The one I told you about."

Oh, shit... Razielle wasn't the one who had to worry about her relationship. It was me.

CHAPTER 10

I never expected to be meeting the ex-girlfriend. I'd thought she was gone for good. Devon had told me a little bit about her early in our relationship, but barely a word since then. So much time had passed, I hadn't connected the dots from when Ivanic was talking about her at lunch yesterday. She was a wolf shifter who'd graduated from here a few years ago and gone to university in Canada. I should have remembered.

"I'm sorry. I should go," Clara said. "I said what I came here to say. I'll see you in class, Maeve."

"Since you'll be around, we should catch up," Devon offered. "It's been too long." He glanced at me. "The three of us should grab something to eat this weekend."

"I have commitments at home this weekend, but maybe some other time," Clara said, then gave an awkward smile—something I hadn't thought she'd be capable of—and headed toward the Manor ahead of Devon and me.

"We should all grab something to eat?" I asked. "You should catch up? Did you seriously just say that?"

"Yeah? I didn't want you to think I was going behind your back," Devon said, considering how hard he wanted to defend his statement. "We're just friends. That's all. You have nothing to worry about."

It was just the thing someone with ulterior motives would say. "I'm not worried," I said, just the thing a worried person would say.

"Good," Devon said. "Because I love you and no one else."

I simply nodded and smiled—a not overly amused smile—and I also refused to give him the reassurance by saying it back. "What are you doing here, anyway?"

"I came to check on you. Make sure you made it to our training session okay."

"How very thoughtful of you."

"I thought so." He gave me a wry grin, again trying to lighten the mood. "What was Clara talking to you about?"

"Making some clarification about the prediction made in Divination this morning," I said as we started to make our way toward the Manor, now that Clara was out of sight. "Nothing really."

"What was the prediction?"

"That I would be attacked," I said with a shrug. "Which is kind of like a daily occurrence for me with Combative Casting and all. So, whatever. It was nothing."

"And the professor wasn't concerned? Who is it? Professor Lin?"

"Yeah. I mean no, she wasn't concerned." I could feel the warmth at my chest. "I mean who's left to attack me? You and your mother are no longer after my needle. Tarquin's dead. The plague vampires are dead. I know I'm good at making enemies, but think I'm good for now."

"If you and the professor aren't concerned, then I'm not concerned," Devon said as we made our way up the front steps of the Manor. At the top, he held the door open for me.

On our way to the stairs, we passed the entrance of the Memorial Hall. I stopped and stared at the eulogy collages of kind words and moving pictures on the walls. It was hard to believe we'd only been introduced to it yesterday. These past few days had felt like weeks—or even months.

"Have you been through it yet?" I asked Devon, who'd taken my hand and was already urging me toward the stairs.

"I heard about it."

"Then you heard what they did?" I pulled my hand away. "Nym's on the wall, remembered as one of the fallen students—one of the casualties of last year's atrocity. It's not right."

"I agree. It's not," Devon said, taking my hand again, but not tugging me forward. "However, there are those in the administration that still believe vampires should not be permitted in Spellcrest. The events of last year only exacerbated that belief."

"Does your mother feel that way?"

Devon shook his head. "She's not a fan of vampires, but she's not the enemy."

"Well, is she going to do anything about it?"

"I don't know."

"She'd better," I insisted. "Because those students deserve better."

Devon didn't say anything more, probably weighing his options as to whose good side it was better to be on—mine or his mother's.

As much as I wanted to, I couldn't blame him for being cautious. He had been for as long as I'd known him. I was the one jumping headfirst out of windows without a plan.

We left Memorial Hall and made our way up to the fifth floor, where the semi-secret entrance to the headmistress's office was. I wasn't a lowly neophyte anymore, embarrassingly trying to solve a Harry Potter riddle to locate the elusive office door. Now, I'd been there more times than most students. And I'd seen things in that office I wished I could forget.

After pulling the door into existence, we climbed

the spiral staircase and emerged through the hole in the floor, a design inspired by the lonely tower, no longer looming in the distance.

As expected, Headmistress Christi was seated on the far couch, her attention on her phone until she noticed us enter the office.

"For a moment, I almost thought you'd lost your way," she said, placing her phone on the coffee table and folding her hands in her lap. "How are you feeling after another day in the unrestrained simulator?"

"I'm alive," I said, snapping more than intended. Memorial Hall had soured my mood, and I couldn't let the insensitivity stand. "What are you going to do about the names in Memorial Hall of people who are still alive? My friend, Nym, is among them. Haven't they been through enough?"

"I understand you're upset," the headmistress said. "Adding the turned students to the wall was not in the approved plans. The next academy board meeting is next week, and I've already added it to the agenda."

"Can't you just say the word and get it changed now? You're the headmistress, for God's sake." I stood defiantly on the opposite side of the coffee table with my arms crossed.

"I know you're headstrong about getting what you want done in the moment, but as you progress into the real world—the non-magical and magical world alike—you'll need to learn to go through proper channels. You can't just do everything yourself. Some things you'll need approval for. Some things you'll need help with. Strength alone will not get what you want done. Leadership and diplomacy will also be required in many instances. Why don't you take a seat? Childish intimidation tactics will not get you the desired outcome any faster."

Devon placed a hand at the small of my back and nudged me forward.

"I'm going. I'm going," I said, exasperated, and took a seat on the adjacent couch. Devon sat next to me, though he kept some distance. "What happens if the board doesn't vote to remove my friend's name from the wall?"

"We'll cross that bridge when we come to it," Headmistress Christi said. "We're not going to worry about the undesired outcome now. Do you think like that when you're trying to summon your powers?"

"No," I said. "If I did, then it wouldn't work."

"Precisely," she said with a knowing smile. "Then don't do it now."

She still had a way of making me feel like a neophyte, even though I was the same age as her son, who'd graduated two years ago. Over the past trimester, he'd been getting more training than I had because he didn't have the same class load to uphold. I had started out with better control of my needle and seamstress powers, but that was no longer the case. Devon had years on me with his traditional magical abilities, so he picked up his new tailor abilities with greater ease. He was practically my coach again, though the headmistress hadn't specifically assigned him as such.

"Do you want to tell me anything about your simulation experiences?" Headmistress Christi asked. "Now that you've gotten the issue with your friend off your chest, I suspect you're having to battle through your parents' first deaths. How is that playing out?"

"Yes," I said, not really wanting to talk about this. "It's been difficult, to say the least."

"And have you had the opportunity to battle any vampires?"

I shook my head.

"Good. Then they're not as much of a phobia as with many of the other students. I'm sure your experiences last year had something to do with that. I understand these are personal demons to conquer, but it can be therapeutic to talk about. If not with me, then with someone." She glanced at Devon as she spoke.

"I've offered my support and will continue to do so," Devon chimed in. "Maeve knows I'm always here for her."

"As am I," the headmistress said, offering a warm smile that looked almost unnatural on her. "I remember my own simulations. This was many years ago now. But they will stick with you. They will define you. At times, they may seem cruel, but they will make you strong. You will come to know yourself better and what you're capable of."

"Is it true a student died in the simulation?" I asked. I didn't want to immediately say I'd heard it from Devon, so left out that minor detail.

"It is," Headmistress Christi admitted without pause. "Did you hear it from Professor Ocumulus? I wouldn't think it the best time for telling such stories."

"He didn't tell it to the class. I heard it in passing."

"Timothy Nesenoff. It was very unfortunate. It happened in my sapient year. I'd shared the class with him, along with others."

"Was he a friend of yours?"

"I didn't know that," Devon said, sounding genuinely surprised. "Why did you never mention it before?"

"I don't know. Perhaps I didn't think you were ready to hear it."

"And I am now?"

"You both are." She took a moment to gather her thoughts. "Timothy Nesenoff. If it hadn't been for what happened, there's no way I would have remembered his name all these years. Despite all the classes we shared, I'd only talked to him a handful of times. He was quiet and only had a few friends. He spent much of his time alone with his nose in a book.

"Professor Daniel Ocumulus, the late brother of our current Professor Ocumulus, ran the Combative Casting Three class on his own that day. However, he was cleared of any wrongdoing. Timothy's body wasn't removed from his simulation pod until all the students were out of the classroom. As quickly as we were ushered out, those of us who still had to pass the pod were able to see him lying unresponsive on the floor. We didn't know he was dead at the time, though most of us thought as much. It wasn't until later that we received the official announcement.

"The simulations were stopped for half the trimester as the professors worked diligently to ensure the safety of all Spellcrest students. As you can imagine, no one wanted to step foot inside the pods after an event like that. Even though it turned out to be a fluke, everyone feared for their own lives."

"What happened to him?" I asked. "Why did he die?"

"He had a rare heart condition that wasn't disclosed and suffered a heart attack from the extraordinary stress of the simulation. The situation revealed a great weakness in the safety protocols. Once he was found, he was dead too long, unable to be revived. The pods are much more advanced now —many upgrades made over the years."

"So, something like that can't happen again?"

"It hasn't happened since. I won't make a blanket

statement to say it can't or won't happen again, but it's highly unlikely given current safety protocols," the headmistress said and reversed the cross of her legs. "You should feel reassured that every time you step into a simulation pod, you will make it out alive. Perhaps your body won't always feel it will, but you'll objectively know you're okay and the pain is only in your head."

"I feel *so* reassured," I said, sarcastically.

"Do you have a bad heart you forgot to tell me about?" Devon joked, though it seemed in bad taste.

I didn't call him out on it. "If I did, with all the shit I've been through, it would have given out by now."

"I think we should move on," the headmistress interjected. "Time to get back to your training. Remember, not all the monsters you meet are in a simulation. Many are out in the real world— different times, different worlds—trying to destroy all we hold dear, right here and now."

"You certainly don't need to remind me of that. I've seen plenty destroyers already."

"I just want to make sure you remember the immense responsibility of a seamstress." Head-mistress Christi took a deep breath, her expression darkening. "It's a calling that must be answered. But it should be a choice to the one called to answer. I know you didn't receive a choice when you were given the gift… but you should have been."

"Are you trying to take my needle from me again?" I snapped.

"No, my dear," she said, sadly. "Quite the contrary. I have faith that you'll be an unstoppable seamstress when you're older—an unstoppable team, the two of you. But is this what you truly want? The dangers you've found yourself in during the past few years since being given your needle is representative to the life of a seamstress. Sometimes, you find the danger, and in other times the danger finds you. Is that the life you want?"

"How can you ask me that now? After all I've been through…"

"It is precisely why I'm asking. The life of a seamstress is a life of service and sacrifice."

"Mother, if you know Maeve at all, then you know how much she's sacrificed already," Devon said, sounding about as irritated as I was feeling.

"I *do* know," the headmistress said. "I've always known how extraordinary she was—she is. I just want her to know she has a choice. It wasn't right that she wasn't given a choice initially, so I'm doing my best to correct that mistake now."

"Why? It's not like it was *your* fault," I said, though a lot of other things were.

I could blame Headmistress Christi for plenty of things, but forcing me into the seamstress role wasn't one of them.

She looked momentarily unsure of how to

respond. She looked distant, traveling in her head like she'd done to countless worlds, to which her many totem chess pieces could attest.

"I am the head of the Continental Seamstress Council," she finally said. "We are one unit and all share in blame or guilt. It is just as much my fault as it was... Helena's..." She paused. "So, even though it is long overdue, I'm offering you the choice you should initially have received."

All those memories of my introduction to magic were still so vivid, from stumbling upon Helena in a Hollywood front yard to me insisting to Otis that I wouldn't leave my brother behind to attend the premier magical academy in the country. And the thought of Otis—from who he was to me then to who he was to me now—made my heart hurt. If I gave up my needle now, it would feel as if everything I'd been through for the past two and a half years was for nothing.

"If I hadn't been given the needle, would I be at Spellcrest now? If it wasn't for my needle, would I have ever gotten an invitation?" I asked, though I knew the answer despite however the headmistress replied.

"I'm not going to lie to you," the headmistress said, choosing her words carefully. "You probably wouldn't. I will admit now that I had too much animosity toward your mother to grant your admittance even with the contributions her family had made to the academy. That's why you did not receive an invitation when you really were a freshman.

"Your mother and I have since healed our relationship, and you are here now, so ultimately, everything worked out. You're correct in thinking that the needle got you here, but it is no longer necessary for you to stay. No one will stop you from graduating from this fine magical institution."

"I'm not giving up my needle," I proclaimed, taking a moment to glance back at Devon, then returning my full attention to the headmistress. "Helena may not have given me a choice, but she gave me this needle for a reason. It got me here and has opened so many doors. There's no way I'm giving it up now."

Headmistress Christi smiled. "Very well. Per your own admission, you are proceeding purely by your own choosing."

"Yes."

"Then let's continue your training." The headmistress was suddenly possessed with a burst of energy and vigor as she rose from the couch to retrieve her beacon candle.

CHAPTER 11

*H*eadmistress Christi lit the vanilla-scented candle, which she had placed on the coffee table before us. The walls of the tower office faded, illuminating the space with the dimming evening light. The sitting area was awash in the warm orange glow of the flickering candle flame. The sweet scent of vanilla filled my nostrils.

This was the beacon candle she'd been using with us since the beginning of the year. Instead of us each carrying a totem to our transported destination, we'd use the sensory experience of the lit candle to find our way back to this spot. Each time we performed the action, it became more natural and automatic. The focus was on the candle and the feeling of sitting before it rather than trying to envision an entire room, which I'd been doing for the past few years of haphazardly teleporting. The beacon candle also eliminated the chance of losing a given totem in a dangerous situation.

The headmistress didn't seem as enthusiastic about using totems as she used to be. However, perhaps that was only for our training. Or perhaps she simply wanted us to be open to other options and ideas.

"Close your eyes," the headmistress instructed. "Is the beacon clear in your mind?"

"Yes," Devon and I both said, seated side by side on the couch.

"Now, attach yourself to the anchor and reach out to the nearest open seam you can feel. Even though it is not a natural tear, you know to approach it with caution. As safe as it appeared when I created it, there is always the opportunity of compromise. The longer it is open, the greater the chance of someone else finding it."

Apparently, she thought I'd forget everything I'd learned over the Christmas holiday. Headmistress Christi reported each seam she opened to the Continental Seamstress Council, so no other seamstresses would interfere with our training.

"Understood," I said, primarily to pacify her. Devon didn't feel the need to respond.

"Can you feel the seam to which I am referring?"

Like my ability to sense other needles, seams felt like a tug on my soul. I wasn't able to picture or discern a location but go to where the tug took me.

Like my brief training with Dawn—which was really a desperate search for the Plague Staff—the more I was aware of the pulling sensation, the better I was able to recognize it, as well as the direction in which it was leading me. I was led to many dead ends until I'd better developed the skill. Then it was more or less a straight shot.

With teleporting, I had to be more careful—more confident that I was headed in the right direction. And since the headmistress still did not permit seams on campus, the ones she opened were always off academy grounds.

The hardest thing at this point was discerning needles from seams, to make sure I was headed toward the right thing.

"I think so," I said. I could feel Headmistress Christi's and Devon's needles, clear and distinct. The Plague Staff and few seam daggers located on campus provided more vague feelings, which required me to locate and identify.

Yes, I have them all accounted for.

This left me with the last pull, which I'd yet to identify. It was the open seam—the thing I needed to place all my focus on.

"Reach for it and see where it leads," she said.

"I've got it," Devon said.

Show off. I was feeling rusty after my few weeks off. It was amazing how quickly my skills faded. I should have been practicing on my own.

"Very good, Devon. Where are you, Maeve? Have you located the seam?"

"You can take my hand," Devon offered, and soon, I was feeling his warm touch wrapping my fingers.

"No," I said, batting his hand away. "I can do this on my own." I thought back to when he'd needed my help to reach the catacombs—back when my skills had been more refined than his. Those days were gone.

Focus, Rhodes! Recalling memories was not how I was going to locate the seam. And I needed to locate the seam because I sure as hell wasn't going to be someone's teleportation passenger.

The headmistress asked me again, but I was no longer listening to her. My mind was no longer in the tower office. It had gone in search of the open seam, progressing through the darkness as the pull became more pronounced. This told me I was headed in the right direction.

The headmistress knew better than to distract me now. She let me continue to work in peace.

The pull toward the open seam became stronger as my attention zipped through the darkness. It felt farther than the previous trainings, but I couldn't determine how far. Finally, I could feel its electric charge as if I was standing right next to it.

"I'm there," I said, my eyes remaining closed.

"Good, Maeve," Headmistress Christi said. "Then you know what to do."

I did. The next step was to go to it—and to do it without opening another seam. There was always an inherent danger with opening seams, so it was best to use them in this world as little as possible. However, access to other timelines and worlds required the use of seams.

I let the essence of the seam be my guide to transport me to the right location.

Suddenly, I'd broken from my spot in the tower office and was standing in an open meadow, with Devon already beside me.

The seam was a shimmering blue gash in the air, a few feet from the ground. The edges radiated the bright blue light, but the center was a black void darker than space.

The grass beneath our feet was overgrown, sticking up out of the snow. A wall of trees extended behind us and turned at an angle to cut off the meadow to the west. On the other two sides was open air. We were still on a mountain, as high up as Spellcrest.

Other crests and clouds were clear in the distance. The sun had sunk behind the trees, giving the sky a gradient color from black to orange.

But something about this open meadow was familiar. "I feel as if I've been here before."

"You have. We both have," Devon said. "This is

the clearing for Manor West. It's beyond reach now. I don't know when it will be reopened. But it's still here. Would you like to do the honors or shall I?"

"If you've got a coin, we can flip for it," I said with a sly smile.

"I have no problem with you doing it. Go right ahead."

"Now you're just saying I need the practice." I placed my hands on my hips and arched an eyebrow.

"That's not what I'm suggesting at all," Devon argued. "Fine, I'll do it. I have no issue with that, either."

"But maybe I want to do it."

"Oh my God! Do it already!"

I started laughing, which prompted him to start laughing.

"You're impossible," he said, stepped toward me, then planted his full lips on mine.

"One of the many reasons why you love me," I said once we parted from the kiss. "Do you want to sew up the seam?"

"No," Devon said, emphatically. He threw his hands up in the air in surrender. "I most certainly do *not*."

"Well, if you insist." I used my sweetest voice and smiled in victory.

Devon took a few steps back as I approached the open seam. I'd seen many and opened numerous myself, but they still carried a sense of awe and wonder, as well as a dash of terror from not knowing what existed on the other side. Seams were powerful doorways that demanded respect. They were never to be underestimated. If I didn't know who created it, then there was the possibility that it could lead anywhere—or *any when*.

I pinched my forefinger to extract my needle, which appeared on demand now. The needle also moved through my flesh without the slightest discomfort, a big difference from when I first received it. I remembered how much I used to loath needles, cursing the masochist who'd created this supremely magical tool.

I pulled out the needle and the unbreakable red thread flowed from my finger like a thin stream of weightless blood. And once I had enough slack, I started to sew. I punched the needle into the open air next to the seam, where it disappeared, then emerged from the opposite side. When I pulled it tight, the topmost section of the seam closed and became one with the open air. I continued to stitch with ease, watching as the seam vanished inch by inch. Once I reached the bottom, the shimmering blue was extinguished.

"There. Did I miss any spots?" I asked, stepping back to observe the open space where the seam had been.

"Can you still feel it?" Devon asked.

"Sort of." I looked closer at the space where the

seam had been, searching for any glint of the blue light still showing through. But I didn't see anything. It looked as if I'd done a thorough job. "I feel something, but don't think it's the seam."

"I don't feel it," Devon said. "Maybe you're just sensing me."

I gave him an agitated glare. "It's not you. I know what *you* feel like—you know what I mean," I quickly corrected.

"Then what is it?"

"I don't know." I widened my search from the spot where the seam had been, overlooking the meadow and the line of trees in the distance. Then at the edge of the forest, I saw a pair of yellow eyes like two small lanterns in the shadows. We were not alone.

"Over there," I said, pointing to what I began to make out as a wolf.

Upon noticing it had been spotted, the wolf didn't shrink back into the shadows, but stepped away from the trees and stalked into the meadow. The creature that emerged from the forest was no natural animal, but one of the nightmarish werewolves we'd fought on numerous occasions.

"Where there's one, there are usually more," Devon said, scanning the tree line. "We should go."

"Weren't they like the guardians of Manor West or something?" I asked, also looking for more wolves, but not seeing any others. "Shouldn't it know us as S&S members… or at least you? I guess I'm not really one."

"Manor West isn't here anymore. I have no idea where this wolf's allegiance lies. But I don't think we should stick around to find out." Devon grabbed my arm. "Let's get out of here."

"Agreed," I said and found Devon's hand. Going together seemed like a good plan this time. I wasn't so proud to accept help in a dangerous situation.

With my eyes closed, I began to reach for the beacon—the vanilla-scented candle from the head-mistress's office. But sudden barking coming from the wolf cut through my concentration. I also heard the creature picking up speed, unsure if it was still on four legs or had transformed to two. I had to see how much time we had, so I opened my eyes.

The wolf was sprinting toward us, continuing to bark and growl—making as much threatening noise as it could—as if it knew it was ruining our focus.

I could feel the candle, but it was faint. With my focus divided, I wasn't doing enough to transport us, leaving Devon to do all the work.

However, the wolf was coming fast, crossing the meadow with supernatural speed. "Devon, we're not gonna make it!" I yelled, ripping my hand from his and bracing for the attack.

Devon turned and placed both hands on the sides of my head. "Yes, we are. Block out the noise and focus! It's all part of the training!" His voice was shaky.

Clearly, he didn't believe everything he was saying, but I complied by closing my eyes, returning my focus to the lit candle in the tower office.

We can do this, I told myself.

Suddenly, the snarling sounded as if mere feet away. But I couldn't split my focus again. I had to stay the course no matter what happened.

Then the smell of vanilla was overpowering. I was no longer standing in crusty snow, but hardwood flooring. The incredible noise coming from the wolf quickly diminished, as did an anguished cry from Devon.

My eyes shot open, and I gasped when I saw Devon was not standing beside me. My frantic movements startled the headmistress, who'd once again been reading on her phone.

"What's the matter?" she asked.

"Devon… he's still there with the werewolf!" I cried. "I have to get back!"

"A werewolf?" Headmistress Christi sprang from the couch, dropping the phone to the cushions beside her. "Stay here."

She was gone in a flash. I didn't even have a chance to blink… or argue or grab her hand before she ditched me.

My fury surely matched Razielle's with all the times I'd ditched her for her own good. I silently apologized to her before picturing the scene from which I'd just departed. I had a stronger emotional pull to the scene than to Devon or the headmistress separately.

I didn't transition as fast as the headmistress, but a few seconds later, I was once again standing in the mountaintop meadow. However, I wasn't greeted with sounds of a struggle.

Beyond the persistent wind, I could hear nothing else. Besides me, the only other person in the meadow was headmistress Christi. No Devon and no wolf.

CHAPTER 12

"Where is he?" I demanded, assuming the headmistress knew something I didn't.

"Devon was already gone when I arrived," she said.

"And the wolf?"

She gestured to the empty meadow. "As you can clearly see, the wolf—or werewolf—was gone too. You still have a difficult time following directions."

"So I've been told."

She closed her eyes. "Now, shut up. I need to find him."

I was ready to return some harsh words but restrained from doing so. This was a mother, worried about her son. I wanted him back just as badly, but knew she presented the better chance of finding him faster. I fought the urge to interrupt.

While the headmistress was in a deep meditation, I surveyed the meadow for other signs of an attack. If another creature came sprinting from the trees, I had to be ready.

Headmistress Christi's eyes shot open. "I found him."

"Where is he?" I asked, but instead of answering, she simply offered her hand.

I eagerly took it and instantly found myself standing in a dark hallway of stone. I didn't know the specific hallway, but I'd been in the Manor basement enough times to recognize the general aesthetic.

The headmistress manifested a glowing orb to illuminate our surroundings more greatly. Again, it was quiet, but I braced myself for another attack. However, when I saw Devon hunched over against the wall, any surrounding danger left my awareness.

Headmistress Christi cautiously glanced around while I rushed to Devon's side. When I dropped to my knees, I noticed blood on his shirt.

Not a few drops, but nearly soaking through the material.

"Devon, you're hurt!" I cried, wanting to touch him, but not knowing where to safely rest my hand.

"It looks worse than it is. I'm already healing," he said, though his breath still sounded labored. There were parallel slits in his shirt like he'd been clawed across the chest.

"Where's the creature?" Headmistress Christi asked from behind.

"I locked him up." Devon pointed down the hall. "In there."

My gaze followed his finger and quickly realized we were in the hallway with the cells—ones in which I'd been detained several times before.

"This one?" the headmistress asked, walking up to a large metal door.

"Yes. But mother, be careful. He's deadly fast."

"I can handle werewolves."

"He was no werewolf," Devon said. "I thought it was… but… he transformed into a regular man. I didn't get a good look at him. He was wearing a hood. And he moved *so* fast."

"Well, let's see who our mysterious wolfman is," the headmistress said and didn't hesitate to unlock and open the great metal door. However, once the door was open, she didn't utter a word. Then she stepped into the cell without making a sound, leaving the door wide open.

My eyes were glued to the open doorway, expecting to hear something—an exchange of words, a struggle—at any moment. But there was nothing.

"It's too quiet," Devon said.

"And I don't like the sound of it," I answered. "Are you sure you're alright? What happened?"

"I'm fine." Devon was about to continue when

Headmistress Christi emerged from the cell with a frustrated expression. "What is it?"

"The cell is empty," she said. "I made sure he wasn't just hiding inside—out of sight—but he wasn't. He's gone."

"Dammit," Devon muttered. "I was sure this would work. Very few people can escape the spell on these cells." He glanced at me upon voicing the last sentence.

"You underestimated what your foe was capable of, and in doing so, you brought him into the academy." The headmistress closed the door, then returned her attention to us. "Now, you must alert security of the intruder to ensure he isn't still on campus. Do you remember any distinguishing features? Anything that could help identify him?"

"He was tall—six foot three, maybe six foot four... He was dressed in dark colors, nearly black. Thin, like his wolf form. Like I said, his coat had a hood. It was up and shrouded his face in shadows, especially in the dwindling light outside. His black coat was zipped up to his chin. His clothes were unremarkable."

"He transformed from a wolf to a man, and remained fully clothed?" I asked. "How does that work? Wouldn't he have been naked?"

"I suspect he isn't a true shifter," the headmistress said. "His shape as a wolf is an illusion, not a true form."

"Oh, wow… I didn't know that was possible."

"So many things are *possible*."

"I've heard about it, but never seen anyone able to do it so convincingly," Devon said and carefully tried to rise. He placed a hand on the stone wall for support as he slowly got to his feet. "I'm sorry for bringing him here."

"Why didn't you come back with me?" I asked. "If I made it, you should have been able to also."

"Instead of fighting to get us both back, I pushed you along," Devon said. "We were both having a hard enough time concentrating. I thought I could handle him."

"We both could have." I frowned.

"Neither of you should have," Headmistress Christi interjected. "You should have both come straight back. Then I could have dealt with the threat efficiently."

"We closed the seam. That should count for something."

"Maeve did," Devon said. "I won't take credit."

"Yes. There were successes and failures with today's training," the headmistress said bluntly, sounding very much like her old self. That was the headmistress who loved to give me shit. "Devon, do you need help with your healing?"

Devon shook his head. "I'm good."

"Then go enlist security to help find our escaped wolfman. I don't want him freely roaming the campus. If our luck continues, then he's already gone. Let me know what you find."

"What about me?" I asked.

"Our training is done for today," the headmistress answered. "You may have some extra study time."

Yeah, like I'm going to use my extra time for studying. "Or grab an early dinner."

"If you so desire." The headmistress didn't sound particularly enthusiastic about my response. "Let's head back. This is a restricted area."

I seemed to have gotten myself into a lot of restricted areas over the years. Sometimes, on accident, but often on purpose. I headed upstairs with Devon and Headmistress Christi, where we all headed in different directions. Even after all we'd been through, Devon still wasn't overly comfortable showing too much affection in front of his mother.

He promised to catch up with me later, then was gone.

I was left alone in the entrance of the Manor.

From this central spot, I could see the entrance and exit of Memorial Hall. Just the sight of it brought back all the frustrating memories from earlier in the afternoon.

The headmistress said she'd do something about the vampire students on the walls, but I didn't trust she'd really fight for it. I'd learned that Miss Long was Devon's ex-girlfriend—and he'd wanted all of us to hang out! Even though he said there were no longer any romantic feelings between them, how could I be sure?

If I wasn't careful, I could inadvertently drive him right into her arms.

And Razielle thinks she's the one with the problem.

I tried not to picture them together, but my mind naturally went there. They must have been quite the power couple on campus. The thought made me sick to my stomach.

And then there was the warning from Miss Long, in which she'd tracked me down to specifically tell me the reading from class had been wrong. I was going to be attacked.

Holy shit! I was attacked! Well, Devon and I were. I supposed that still counted.

Was that it or was my real attack still coming? With the wolfman still at large, I had no way of knowing. The best thing I could hope for would be Devon finding him and putting him behind bars. Until then, the question would remain open.

CHAPTER 13

"*I* don't think you have a worry about Ivanic falling for our wolf shifter TA," I said to Razielle as we headed back to Shadow Peaks Hall after a relatively quiet dinner. Nym hadn't wanted to join us and Ivanic left early to catch up on Multi-World History reading—though Razielle's cold shoulder may have contributed to him wanting to escape.

"And why do you say that?" Razielle asked, skeptically.

"Because Devon already did."

She stopped and stared at me. "What the hell are you talking about?"

"Miss Long is Devon's ex-girlfriend. She graduated a year ahead of him and broke up with him upon leaving for university."

"So, you're like his rebound."

"I wouldn't call it that," I said, making a face at the flippant comment.

"Then what would you call it?"

"Just another relationship, not a rebound. It had been months since they'd broken up, not days."

"It doesn't have to be days," Razielle said. "If he was still pining after her when you two got together, then you're a rebound."

"Whatever. He *wasn't* still pining after her."

"I'm sure he wasn't." She was seeing me getting upset and trying to get back on my good side. "So, if Ivanic isn't what I'm destined to lose in the coming weeks, then what is it?"

I shrugged. "But if you keep giving me shit, it could quite possibly be me."

"No, that can't be it," Razielle said without giving it a moment's thought and started walking again. Despite my current agitation, she was right. "Still… It's gonna bug me as to what it could be. At least you got an easy one. You'll be tested. That's like every damn day in the simulator."

"Yeah… No mystery there," I said. I hadn't mentioned my run in with the wolfman in the forest —or that the initial reading I'd been given was wrong. Hopefully, Devon would find the guy and we could all move on.

"You always get lucky."

I didn't want to remind her of all the ways her

statement was patently false. If it was made with complete sarcasm, then I could jump on board.

"I'll have to remember to thank my lucky stars," I said.

"Oh!" she exclaimed, catching me off guard. "Maybe you being tested isn't about the simulation, but your relationship will be tested because of Devon's history with Miss Long."

I rolled my eyes. My reading wasn't actually a *test*, but an *attack*. And I wasn't afraid of Devon attacking me. "I'll assume it's not a test of our relationship. That okay with you?"

"I'm just trying to look out for you," Razielle said.

Her *looking out for me* felt like poking me with needles—and not with the magical kind. But I let the comment go with a sense of maturity I was still getting used to. It didn't come naturally, but at least I could now stop myself from lashing out at every comment that pissed me off. And marginally fewer comments were pissing me off these days.

Once inside, the main entrance of Shadow Peaks Hall was a large sitting area where students read and did homework by the warmth of the oversized fireplace. I always scanned the students in the room before heading upstairs. This time, I noticed Ivanic sitting by himself, quietly reading from a tablet.

"You look enthralled," I said, suddenly standing over his shoulder and startling him. Razielle appeared by my side and let out a snort of laughter, which garnered disapproving glances from others studying in the room.

"I'm fighting to stay awake," Ivanic said. "I don't care how many worlds are covered in the course; history is still boring."

"Then it's time for you take a break, my love," Razielle said and snatched the tablet out of his hand.

He gave her a wary look, unsure of how to take her current playfulness after the precarious dinner. "Okay." His word sounded more like a question than acceptance.

"Dessert always lifts her mood," I said, trying to keep my voice low. "You should know that."

"I do." He didn't sound any surer of the situation, but he rose from the cushiony chair. "Can I have my Kindle back now?"

Razielle returned his device and slipped her hand in his as though everything in their relationship was peachy. Ivanic eyed me suspiciously, as if I'd hexed his girlfriend or something equally absurd, as we left the sitting room and headed for the stairs.

Razielle ditched me for her anxious boyfriend—them heading to his room and me returning to ours.

I found our vampire elf roommate lying on her bed, staring blankly at the ceiling. Her hands were folded over each other, resting on the center of her chest. If her eyes hadn't moved when I entered, I might have had the momentary thought she was dead.

"Whatcha doing?" I asked, taking a seat on the edge of my bed and facing her.

"Counting my heartbeats," Nym said, her voice soft and anguished.

"Fully turned vampires still have a heartbeat, don't they? I mean, I know they don't in the movies, but—"

"Yes, but it's not the same. It beats differently. I'm sure it feels different. I want to feel mine for as long as I can. I want to remember how it feels."

"You're going to be okay," I assured her, but she immediately snapped back at me.

Nym shot up with lightning speed, her eyes fiery. "You don't know that! You don't know anything about what I'm going through!"

Whoa! The fangs were coming out—figuratively, at least for the moment.

"You're right. I'm sorry," I said, trying to pacify her and keep her from attacking me. Maybe *she* was the one my Divination reading warned me about. I didn't really believe the thought, but couldn't deny it as a possibility. "But Razielle and I are here to help you in any way we can, even if it's just to listen."

Nym scooted back on the bed and placed her back against the wall. Her movements were erratic, not graceful like she used to be, as she adjusted to her increasing speed.

"I'm getting hungrier," she said.

"Well, you did skip dinner. We can go back. Just you and me."

"No, you don't understand," she said, shaking her head. "Regular food doesn't help. No matter how much I eat, I still feel hungry. Even when I overeat and feel sick, I'm still hungry."

"I'm sorry. That sounds terrible," I said.

"In my concentration class…" Nym stopped, seemingly unable to finish the sentence.

"It's okay. You can tell me."

"Blood was brought in for us." She could no longer look me in the eyes, apparently ashamed of what she was about to say next. It was clear where her story was going. "We were all given the opportunity to drink. We weren't forced to or anything. It was a choice. All the others did. I was the only one who didn't."

"Well, that's good. Isn't it?"

"I didn't want it… but was so hungry. Like I said, none of the food I was eating would fill me up." Nym paused again, looking anywhere else in the room except for at me. "I finally asked for it. All it took was a sip. I couldn't help myself from drinking it all. And as gross as it made me feel emotionally, it was actually making me feel better than I had in days. My family didn't want to see me before. This just solidifies them never wanting to see me again."

"That's not true," I said. "I know they haven't exactly been receptive to your transformation, but deep down, I know they still love you. They'll come around. You'll see."

"I don't want to hurt you."

"You're not going to. I'm not afraid of you hurting any of your friends." I stared at her, trying to will her attention toward me. And when it didn't work, I commanded her to do so. "Look at me, little elf."

She didn't immediately comply, but finally gave in to my persistence.

"You're not going to hurt anyone," I said. "Your parents still love you, and they will accept you as you are now. I know the transition's hard, but the self-loathing isn't helping. You'll have to learn to love yourself first. Then the other things will fall into place. You'll see."

"Why did this have to happen to me?"

"Because someone upstairs knew you could handle it."

"Toby said he's not able to make it back to Spell-crest this weekend," Nym said. "I'm afraid he doesn't want to see me."

"I'm sure he's dying to see you," I said, then cringed at my word choice. She didn't react, so I continued talking. "You guys have been together for a whole year. He loves you. He's been there for you every step of the way. You have nothing to worry about."

"Yeah... I guess..."

My phone buzzed in my pocket, so I fished it out and saw a text from Devon.

We didn't find him, but ensured the campus is secure, Devon said.

How can the campus be secure if he's still out there?

He's not on campus and we strengthened the magical barrier. He won't be able to get back on campus without help.

Well, don't help him next time. I ended my message with an emoji with his tongue sticking out.

He didn't take the bait. *I just wanted to give you an update, so you weren't continuing to worry.*

How very thoughtful of you.

"Who is it?" Nym asked.

"It's just Devon saying goodnight," I said.

"You can go. You don't have to stay here keeping me company."

"No. I'm right where I want to be."

It had been a rough couple of days for everyone, but I was genuinely worried for Nym. She seemed to be taking things the hardest of us all. I wished there was a way to stop her transition. But as far as I knew, there was no cure for vampirism. There was no reversal. All I could do—*we could do*—was make sure she didn't have to go through this impossible time in her life alone.

CHAPTER 14

*A*ll of us sapients had somehow made it through our first week of the winter trimester. Finley was having fun telling tales of fighting through the gauntlet. He had no idea what awaited him in the simulation chamber. And much like me, he had a closet overflowing with skeletons ripe for exploiting. This wasn't something I could protect him from, not that I played the role of his protector much anymore. Everyone had to experience the simulations alone.

Sunday evenings were reserved for family dinners, so we all gathered at my parents' townhouse. Mom was still the head of Rainley Hall, but she now employed an assistant house master who lived in the dormitory and was on call during off hours, so Mom no longer had to spend the night there. She could come home in the evenings like a regular job and sleep in her own bed beside her husband. It was clear they were thrilled with the updated arrangement.

Quin and I set the table as my father drained the vegetables and took the vegetarian fajitas out of the oven. Mom was grabbing a bottle of wine for the adults to drink while Finley and Guy were useless as usual, watching television in the other room. Maybe it was better having them out of our way. Too many cooks in the kitchen didn't exactly speed up the process.

"Are the dishes clean?" I asked Mom as she strolled back into the room with a bottle of Pino Grigio.

"No," she said. "We'll run the dishwasher after dinner."

"We need two more forks."

"Why are you telling me when you could be washing them right now? Quin, are you having any wine?"

"Like you even have to ask," Quin said, adding an assortment of condiments to the table.

"I always ask."

"I don't want any," I said.

"I wasn't asking *you*." Then Mom stopped uncorking the bottle and turned to me. "My little girl is going to be twenty in a few months. It's a big accomplishment."

"Yeah, with the trouble I always seem to get

myself into, it's a miracle I've been able to stay alive for twenty years. Though, I guess I shouldn't count my chickens yet."

"It's the forgotten age," Quin said. "You're no longer a teenager, yet you're also not twenty-one. It wasn't much of a milestone to me."

"Every celebrated birthday is an important milestone," Dad said, bringing the steaming pan of fajitas to the table. "Maeve, can you tell the boys it's time for dinner?"

"It's time for dinner!" I yelled.

"I guess I should have expected that." Dad rubbed his ears before returning the potholders to their designated drawer.

"Coming!" Guy yelled back.

"The joys of family gatherings," Mom said, taking her first sip of wine.

"You're the one forcing us to all be here," I said, though *forcing* didn't exactly feel like the right word. When I got my parents back, I'd promised myself I'd never take them for granted again. But at only a year and a half since that fateful day, I seemed to already be falling into the dreadful routine.

"I'm not forcing anyone; I'm encouraging everyone to set aside some special family time. I understand it's hard with competing priorities, but it's important, and important things need to be scheduled."

"I know. I'm sorry. I didn't mean to make our

Sunday dinners sound like such a chore. I honestly love them."

"You love what?" Guy asked as he entered the kitchen with Finley in tow.

"Sunday dinners," Quin said.

"Totally. They provide my best eating for the whole week. I'm ready to dig in!" Guy pulled out the chair in his usual spot—with Quin next to him and Finley across. Mom and Dad took the ends, and I sat next to Finley and adjacent to Dad.

"There should be leftovers," Dad said. "You're always welcome to take some."

"Don't be giving away all of our delicious food," Mom chimed in.

"I can always make more for you, honey." Dad gave her a warm smile and raised his glass of wine. "Cheers, everyone. I'm so thankful we could all be here for another Sunday and to the start of a new trimester for our current Spellcrest students."

"Cheers," everyone chorused before starting to pass the serving bowls.

"Hey, Maeve, you know who I ran into this week?" Finley asked, passing me the bowl of Mexican rice.

"I give up," I said, dropping the large spoonful onto my plate, then passing the bowl to Dad.

"Do you remember Grayson—my original neophyte roommate?"

"Sure. He practically wet himself every time a girl talked to him."

"That's so not true, but whatever. He's back and he's a medial like me. He joined my Combative Casting class. We hung out a bit to catch up."

"He had a real thing for Nym. He should see her now."

"She'd probably rip his head off now," Finley said with a shiver.

"Only if he got on her bad side."

Random conversations continued to circulate around the dinner table. Everyone was in a generally good mood and expressing superficial complaints.

I was the only one coming off a substantially stressful week, but wasn't about to bring everyone else down with my complications.

Mom, Guy, and Quin had all been sapients at Spellcrest, so they knew what I was going through. I had no desire to talk about it with them—especially with Mom.

The other random attack was one of those things I had a knack for manifesting—wrong place at the wrong time. However, the academy security team had the important task of making sure the wolfman wasn't a threat to me or any other student. I trusted they'd be able to handle him, if he ever decided to show his face around here again.

"Well, I've got interesting news," Dad said, addressing the whole table. The other conversations quickly died down. Once the room was quiet, he continued. "Headmistress Christi has reached out to me, with the desire of setting up a meeting with General Cruach. We've had a ceasefire now for over a year, and she is ready to act as the liaison to negotiate a permanent peace treaty with Kicryria."

"I still think you need to be careful," Mom said. "We all know what she's capable of. And she'll be representing the GBMA, and I don't trust any of those bureaucrats any farther than I can throw them."

"I know. But it's a start. It's what we've been working toward."

"I always thought she was one of the strong proponents of the war," Quin said. "Didn't she almost singlehandedly destroy Ogginosh? And now she wants to negotiate peace?"

"She's changed," Dad said. "We all have. Fighting gets old, especially when you start losing the things you love."

"Death has a way of providing perspective," Mom said before taking a bite of her fajita.

"I don't want to get my hopes up, but just opening these discussions could be hugely beneficial."

"Has the GBMA's stance on the accessibility of magic changed?" Guy asked. "They're suddenly willing to give up their coveted status just like that?"

"I don't think it will be quite that easy," Dad

rebutted. "Both sides will have to give—hence, it will be a negotiation."

"It sounds like good news to me," I said, trying to give Dad a little support. He was getting beat up from all sides.

"Thank you, Maeve. I think so too, though I understand everyone's trepidation. We don't know what will come of these initial talks and we still need to find neutral ground, but it's surely a step in the right direction."

Dad released the floor, allowing for separate conversations to quickly arise. Guy and Quin had been spending more time with Dad in Kicryria. Currently, they were working on the rebuilding effort of Ogginosh, a project that had started before the start of the school year, last fall, and had been keeping them busy.

I wished there was something I could do to help, but both my parents insisted I focus on my schoolwork. Most weekends didn't consist of any construction work, so I remained in Spellcrest, taking time to recharge with my friends and Devon.

Devon still insisted he had no lingering feelings for Miss Long, but I couldn't help thinking of them together. Maybe he was telling the truth and I was the crazy, jealous girlfriend. It wasn't as though I'd caught them together since our first encounter. However, every time I texted him, I wondered if she was with him. I couldn't ask. Then he'd *know* how crazy I was. The only time I could be sure was during first period, when I knew exactly where *she* was.

When dinner was finished and the dishes had been cleaned and put away, we all hung out in the living room for an hour or so, then began getting antsy for our own space.

I wished my parents a good night and left with the others.

Quin and Guy's townhouse was halfway to the village, where they dropped out, leaving Finley and me to continue the rest of the way to the dormitories on our own.

"Do you really believe they'll allow magic into the mainstream?" Finley asked as we crunched through the snow covering the village square.

"I don't know," I said. "If they do, then it'll change everything."

"If they do, then I won't be special anymore. I'm barely reaching the point of average here as it is."

"It's all in your head," I said. "If you don't believe you're special, then it won't matter what anyone else says."

"I'm just getting used to the way things are now. I know it sounds selfish, but I don't want things to change again."

"Things are going to change regardless."

I gazed up at the iron gates of Spellcrest Academy as we left the square.

So much had already changed. This school had been through more in the past two years than in the rest of its several-hundred-year history. Some stability would have been nice, but I knew better than to expect it. "Imagine introducing magic to everyone we used to know. Our old friends. Our old housemates—the ones who weren't assholes, anyway."

This made Finley laugh. "You know some of them would want to burn us at the stake."

"I don't doubt it." I laughed. "We all know introducing magic to the world will cause a revolution, but it'll be a good one—at least in the long run. It's what our parents risked their lives for. It's something worth fighting for."

"I hope you're right."

"When have I ever steered you wrong, little man?" I said. "Sorry. I know you hate that."

Finley was quiet for a moment as we continued our trek onto the white, blanketed campus. "Not when we're alone. It reminds me when it was just the two of us. Those days were hard, but many of them were still great. Ya know?"

I nodded. I *did* know. The thing I missed most about those days was the relationship we had. Back then, I never dreamed of anyone coming between us and wedging us apart. We were closer now than we'd been in the past two years, but I couldn't exactly admit we were close—not anymore. I wasn't resentful or bitter—though God knew how long it took me to shake those emotions—just a hole where our ironclad relationship used to be.

We reached Rainley Hall first, where he gave me a quick, formal hug, then we parted ways—probably until next Sunday. The big sister in me still felt the need to wait until my little brother was safely inside. I sauntered the rest of the way to Shadow Peaks Hall, kicking up powdered snow along the way. There was barely a soul outside, most of the students getting ready to turn in for the night and greet a new week.

The study room on the main floor was half filled, but no one I wanted to talk to caught my eye. It was as quiet as a library, the crackling from the flames in the fireplace making the most noise.

From several doors away, I could already hear Razielle talking about something, probably driving Nym crazy with her super sensitive hearing. And when I opened the door, the eccentric Nephilim turned her exuberance on me.

"It happened!" she exclaimed.

"What happened? What the hell are you talking about?" I asked, though I was relieved to interpret her excitement as a good thing.

"My reading! I will lose something close to me within the next moon cycle."

"I take it from this reaction it wasn't Ivanic."

"God no. It was my phone! I couldn't text you

about it because, well, I lost it. I'll have to get a new one tomorrow."

"She dropped it while flying," Nym interjected.

"What have I told you about texting and flying?" I said.

"I know, *Mom*," Razielle sighed. "I'll probably find it once the ground thaws. By that time, who cares. But isn't that great? I was afraid it would be something terrible. I mean, losing my phone does suck, but it's easily replaceable."

"And it's not like it's something completely unexpected. You do have a reputation for going through like ten phones a year."

"And this would be number one for this year," Nym said. She sounded less morose than she had been for most of the week. I guessed she found this little incident amusing as well.

"Check," Razielle. "A new year means a new phone."

"A new month means a new phone for you," I said.

"But isn't this great? My torturous waiting is over! I'm finally free!"

"It's been less than a week."

"Whatever. Don't be a killjoy. I'm free!" Razielle said without losing an ounce of enthusiasm. "And no more readings for me. I hate that Divination shit. That stuff's like a curse. And speaking of curses, what about yours? Anything unexpected?"

"Nope," I lied. "We all know mine is just talking about the simulations."

"So, things are still good between you and Devon?"

"*Yes!* We're fine." My exasperation revealed I was less confident than I was trying to portray.

Luckily, Razielle didn't press. "Then I guess we're both good—or *all good* since Nym was lucky enough not to get a reading in the first place."

"I've got enough of a curse for me, thank you," Nym said. "No need to pile on more."

I didn't have the energy to get into another positive paradigm talk with Nym over what she was calling her curse. The vibe in the room was positive enough, and I didn't want to jinx it.

CHAPTER 15

*I*t took a few weeks, but all of us sapients were finally falling into a comfortable rhythm, a big accomplishment from the hellish start of the trimester. We were all facing our demons, which were becoming less paralyzing and soul-crushing, now truly learning to fight back.

There was no magic formula. Just practice, reinforcement, and determination. Pretty soon we'd be conquering those sadistic bastards.

However, we had a wildcard in the group. The only one I couldn't quite read was Nym. She had her good days and her bad days, so it was difficult to tell what her progress was. Her journey was different than the rest of ours. She was fighting her demons while at the same time coming to terms with her transition. And I didn't think these were necessarily mutually exclusive things. I feared the enemy she was fighting was herself—the version of herself she could become.

I had limited vampire experience, but Mom assured me that there were plenty of good vampires in the world and Nym would surely become one of them. I hoped she was right.

"I DID IT!" Ivanic exclaimed as soon as I walked into Advanced Evocation. He was sitting by himself and obviously dying to tell someone his inspiring news.

"I give up," I said, taking my seat at the table ahead of his. "What did you do? But more importantly, where's Bree?" She shared Combative Casting with Ivanic before this period, so they typically arrived together.

"Not more importantly, but she stopped at the bathroom. She's fine." Ivanic was talking a mile a minute. "I finally did it! I bested my antagonists in the simulation!"

"Are you willing to tell me who they are now that they're not the boogeymen they were a few weeks ago?"

But before he could answer, Erik and Bree strolled into the room. "I did it, buddy!" Ivanic said, slapping the table.

"You got them?" Erik leaned his backpack against one of the table legs. "I knew you were close!"

MICHAEL PIERCE

"Yeah, I just had the feeling that today would be the day… and it was!"

"How about you?" I asked, turning to Bree.

"I don't have such compelling news, but I'm good," Bree said with a shrug. "I'm getting there. It shouldn't be long now."

"Nice work," I said, then turned back to Ivanic. "So, who are they?"

"The alpha's son has his pack of misfits," Ivanic said. "They were older and gave me a hard time because of my family's standing in the pack. Allegations were made against my father when I was just a cub. He was ultimately cleared, but the stigma remained. It was hard through a lot of my early schooling."

"Were they worse in real life or the simulation?"

"The simulation takes what's in your head and intensifies it, like tenfold. Even though there were a lot of threats, it never truly escalated to anything close to what I had to endure in the simulation. And I'd been younger and built it all up in my head. They were only messing with me and threatening me, though at the time, I thought they literally were trying to kill me. In the simulation they were—and they did. But never again."

"They can't touch you now," Erik said. "You'll rip their throats out and then some."

I remembered Ivanic ripping out the throats of the winged men during the first battle of Spellcrest.

The cheerful and carefree guy I'd come to know had disappeared in that moment, consumed by the giant cougar he'd transformed into. With the way he'd jumped into that fight, I was convinced it hadn't been his first time killing something—or *someone*—but I'd never been able to bring myself to ask. Like the rest of us, his scars were received long before setting foot at the academy.

"I'm so happy you were able to conquer your nightmare," I said. "It must really feel great."

"You have no idea—or maybe you do…"

I shook my head. "I'm still working on mine but making worthy progress."

As the class began, Professor Quail instructed us to switch partners again. For the past week, I'd been working with Erik. Now, I was moving on to Ivanic. Next, we'd have to move outside our small circle of friends—not that it mattered because I essentially knew everyone in my grade by this point.

We were still doing a similar exercise with plucking words out of our partner's mind. And today we'd be progressing to short phrases.

Erik and I switched tables, so we could sit next to our new partners. Ivanic already had his hand shielding a small piece of paper, ready to begin writing.

"We're going to keep things PG this time, right?" I asked, sliding another piece of paper closer to me.

"The only rule is *there are no rules*," Ivanic said, glancing up with a smirk.

"Well, I'm keeping myself out of trouble. You can do what you want."

"Thanks for the permission."

However, he did keep his phrase completely innocent, which I guessed in under ten minutes. *Razielle is the best girlfriend in the world*. He also tried to make me promise not to tell her, which I begrudgingly agreed to.

"I don't want her to think she's got me whipped or anything, even though she does," Ivanic said, crumpling up his paper to destroy the evidence.

"At least you admit it," I said with a chuckle. "That's a hell of a lot better than most males your age."

"What can I say, I'm an old soul."

"You're a cougar."

Ivanic beamed, the kind of look that used to make me want to push him away—or dump milk in his lap to cool off his raging hormones. But now, he was focused on Razielle instead of me, about which I couldn't have been happier.

"My turn," he said. "You've got your phrase written, right?"

"Ready and waiting," I said, not that it mattered. I could change my answer with a quick thought, but wouldn't be doing it for Ivanic. He didn't need the same kind of reassurance Bree did.

Or perhaps I'll change my answer to ensure he gets it wrong.

I gave Ivanic a devious smile. "Good luck, cougar boy."

"I thought we were going PG. You picked something I won't want to say aloud, didn't you?"

"Search my dirty mind and see what you find," I said, the words almost sounding musical. I had to admit, it made for a good phrase and I immediately thought of transferring it onto my folded piece of paper.

"Now you're just messing with me," Ivanic said, but he was smiling—willing to play along.

Like Bree, he stared deep into my eyes as though it was going to make the mental extraction easier. Though I supposed he was trying to turn the tables and make *me* uncomfortable.

Fat chance on that.

For the next twenty minutes, Ivanic made several guesses, none of which were on the paper, before or after I made the alteration.

"Come on, it has to be *rise and dine, sunshine*," Ivanic whined. "I keep hearing the phrase and it's something I've never heard before." He stopped and turned his attention to the other table. "Unless it's coming from you?"

"Yeah, like that would be my phrase," Erik said, then laughed, which only frustrated Ivanic further.

MICHAEL PIERCE

I wry smile spread across my lips. "Is that your final answer?"

"I don't know. Is it right?"

"I can't let you know whether or not it's right until you confirm it's your final answer."

Erik and Bree had now stopped their mental exercise, putting Ivanic squarely on the spot. Then out of the corner of my eye, I noticed Professor Quail had taken notice of our table and was now listening in, even though he was still standing several tables away.

Ivanic looked as though he wanted to retreat into his cougar form and either rip the table apart in a display of power or bolt from the room.

"I'm not giving you a hint," I reiterated. "You're a big boy."

I was actually surprised he hadn't heard the phrase he'd extracted from my mind since he'd now been dating Razielle for over a year. I'd heard it from Razielle's housekeeper fairy in our neophyte year, and it had stuck with me ever since.

"Whatever," Ivanic groaned. "Yes. It's my final answer."

I removed my hand from the folded piece of paper set before me and slid it toward him. "Better luck next time," I said, my grin widening.

However, as Ivanic unfolded the paper, his smile grew to match my own. "I knew you'd try to pull something!" he exclaimed and slammed the open paper down in front of me.

My eyes widened at the sight of the *rise and dine, sunshine* phrase written on the paper. *What the hell?*

"Surprised?" Ivanic mocked. "You sure look surprised."

Our friends at the table behind us were enraptured with the developing situation at our table. As was Professor Quail, now weaving his way closer to our table.

"I didn't write that," I said.

"Sure, you did," Ivanic argued. "I just didn't allow you to change it, to change whatever you originally wrote. You gave your hand away by being too cocky. It was obvious you'd try something."

I glanced over at the approaching professor and quietly admitted to what I'd done, hoping to keep it under wraps from the higher authorities.

"Fine. You got me," I said. "You win. I can't take that away from you. Though you must admit, I had you sweating there for a few minutes."

"How are we doing over here?" Professor Quail asked in his irritating sandpaper voice.

"Maeve thinks she's unbeatable, but I bested her," Ivanic said. I was happy—yet not overly surprised— he didn't specifically accuse me of cheating.

"It's not about winning and losing, but about practice and progress," the professor said, then reached for the unfolded paper in front of me. "And

I'm happy to see you're using appropriate classroom language for your exercise."

"I'm all about following the rules," I said, causing the occupants of the table behind me to snicker under their breath.

"Keep up the good work." The professor let the paper float down to the table, then moved on to visit with another team.

"Thanks for not turning me in," I said, once the professor was gone.

"You know I wouldn't do that, despite the awful, horrible, inexcusable thing you did today." Ivanic had his chest puffed out, looking so incredibly happy with himself. "And don't worry, I won't do the same to you. Feel free to lock my paper too."

"No need," I said, covering up the fact I didn't know how to pull off what Ivanic had done. "I trust you."

Ivanic smiled widely, as though he saw right through my words. He knew he'd bested me again.

As powerful as I thought I'd become, today's innocent exercise proved how much I still had to learn.

CHAPTER 16

*E*ven though Ivanic hadn't ratted me out to Professor Quail, he had no qualms about revealing my transgressions to the rest of the group at lunch. Razielle gave me shit for it, but it was obvious she wasn't really offended. I swore it had been the first time I'd done such a deceitful thing, not about to reveal I'd performed a similar action on Bree during the first day of class. However, unlike what I'd attempted with Ivanic, Bree's had been in her favor.

After he'd done his best to make me feel guilty— not that I truly did—Ivanic returned to his real triumph of the day and told the rest of the table of his momentous accomplishment in Combative Casting, having defeated his nemesis for the first time. His story made me hopeful for my upcoming simulation for the first time all year. Ivanic showed the way of what was possible, making a victory believable for the rest of us.

Though I wouldn't admit it aloud, I was slightly irked that I hadn't been the one to succeed first. I was the one with the needle. I was the one with the extra powers only a seamstress could wield. Yet I hadn't been powerful enough to slay my own demons first.

"Today's going to be the day," Razielle proclaimed. "I can feel it. What about you, Maeve? Do you have the boost of confidence too?"

I was about to make a sarcastic comment about *whatever Ivanic can do, I can do better*, but immediately realized that was no longer the case. Deflated, I simply nodded halfheartedly.

"What the hell's the matter with you? You should be stoked!" Razielle admonished my meek response. "You're not gonna win with that attitude."

"I realize that," I said, then glanced at Nym. She was picking at her food, seemingly trying to block out our conversation. She was barely eating these days. She was losing weight, not that she had any spare weight to lose.

"Today's gonna be the day!" Erik exclaimed, wrapping an arm around Sarah's shoulders. "I'm with you!"

"At least someone is," Razielle said.

"I'm with you," I said. "I'm just processing."

"You don't process; you do."

"Yeah she does," Erik said, starting to sound like the old Ivanic.

"Don't make me bitch slap you in front of your girlfriend," I said.

"There she is."

"Do you feel it now?" Razielle asked and chucked a handful of potato chip crumbs at me.

I somehow managed to catch one in my mouth, chewed, swallowed, then produced a victorious grin. "I sure do."

"Finally," Razielle sighed, exasperated. "Take that attitude with you."

The Nephilim's pep talk worked wonders because my invincibility returned as our smaller group of four headed to the basement of Shadow Peaks Hall.

"Nym, I'm going to need a little more energy from you," Razielle said as we entered the large simulation room. "The silent brooding vampire thing isn't working for me. We should all be ready to tear this shit up."

All Nym had to do was shoot our well-meaning roommate her upgraded death glare to let everyone know she was ready and willing to tear anyone to shreds who crossed her path. As much as I wanted her to take that intensity into the simulation, I feared it was her biggest problem.

Nym flashed her fangs, causing Razielle to flinch

and jump back a step. But as soon as she recovered, Razielle hollered in excitement. "That's what I'm talking about!"

"Don't poke the vampire," I said.

"Especially with a wooden stick," Erik added, smugly, careful to keep me between him and a vengeful vampire elf.

Before things could get too out of hand, Professor Ocumulus called the class to order, and after a few questions, instructed us to line up outside our designated simulation pods. I hung my backpack on the hook and placed my crystal and phone inside the small mailbox-shaped locker.

I glanced at Razielle before the direction to enter. She gave me a slow, intense nod, and I returned a thumb's up. Erik got in on the non-verbal exchange, but Nym kept her gaze focused straight ahead into the white abyss of the pod.

I was more confident than I had been in previous sessions, but it was clear I still didn't have the conviction needed to defeat the monsters awaiting me in the simulation world. As much as I wanted my friends to succeed, I didn't want to feel as though I was falling further behind.

You can do this, Rhodes. Rainley. Shit! I can't even give myself a proper pep talk anymore!

I stepped into the pod, got into position, and waited for the virtual world to emerge. Wanting to face the transition head on, I kept my eyes open.

The void of white became pixelated. Dots of various colors appeared all around me, increasing and then blending together to form abstract shapes, which quickly took shape and formed the mountain cabin I'd become so used to. The safe house. The safe word I could finally remember.

Once the new world fully formed, my head was swimming, the dizziness forcing me to stagger to the closest couch and take a breather. This was why I'd closed my eyes since the first day of the school year. I wanted to see if I could better handle the transition now, but discovered I couldn't. It felt like one more setback.

You're not gonna win with that attitude. I wasn't going to win today. That much was plain to see. My simulation hadn't yet begun, yet was already over, done, and gone.

Why face the trial at all today?

I already knew how it was going to end—with me lying a pool of blood, engulfed in flames.

Screw this.

I closed my eyes and sank back into the enveloping couch cushions. My mind instantly recreated the scene that had been haunting me for weeks. My eyes shot open just to escape, needing to be convinced I was still in the deceptive serenity of the safe house.

While I continued to sit and breathe in the virtually enhanced mountain air, the door to the outside world violently swung open and slammed against the adjacent wall. Snow drifted and coated the floor around the open door.

"That's new," I said, tensing up, anticipating someone *or something* to enter the cabin—and invade my sacred safe house.

The door moved inward a few inches then banged into the wall again, repeating the movements in a regular rhythm, as though the cabin itself was breathing.

The world outside the door still matched what I could see through the windows, which was a serene snowy mountain scene. It usually didn't change until I stepped over the threshold. However, the door didn't typically fly open by itself, either.

I didn't know if the cabin itself was going to find a way to push me out, or if the simulation engineers were controlling this part of the experience, with their own protocols with how to urge me out of the safe house and into the simulated world. If I didn't move from my spot on the couch, I figured I was about to find out.

When flames erupted from the far arm rest, there was no doubt that it was my cue to leave. The last thing I needed was to be engulfed in flames in my own safe house.

What happened to this being a sacred space?

I sprang from the couch before it was fully consumed and watched it quickly burn to ash, leaving a dark stain upon the hardwood floor. The fire didn't spread, but instead dissipated with the furniture I'd been sitting on moments ago.

Fine! Not wanting to press my luck any further, I headed for the open door, ready for my parents' death scene to kick my ass again.

To avoid the shock of another transition, I closed my eyes as I passed through the open door continuing to bang against the wall. As expected, my Docs didn't crunch into inches of packed snow. However, I didn't feel as though I'd stepped onto a sidewalk, either. The all too familiar busy street sounds of the southern California town of my youth didn't rise from the forest breeze.

Instead, my feet collided with hard stone. The sounds of my footfalls reverberated around some cavernous room, startling me, and causing my eyes to shoot open.

As terrible as the alley scene was, the newly manufactured scene was even more nightmarish. I was once again in the empty top room of the lonely tower, just as it had been before the vampires took over the academy. There was no dais or line of thrones. No one waiting for me to arrive at all. Just an empty room with silver moonlight shining through the open windows.

I made sure to keep away from the hole in the floor, where the spiral staircase descended to the ground. And as my gaze swept across the stone floor, the true nightmare revealed itself.

Broken angel wings were scattered across the room. Bloody stumps from where the wings had been ripped from angelic bodies were still covered in fresh blood, which continued to ooze and seep through the cracks between the stones.

There wasn't just a pair or two of these horrifying dismembered wings, but dozens of them throughout the room. I could still hear the screams of the plummeting angels after watching Tarquin pluck their wings and toss them from the tower. I could only imagine how many bodies littered the snow around the base of the lonely tower. A tower surrounded by death.

I remained in my spot, several feet from the closest feathered appendage, hypersensitive to any potential movement from the perimeter shadows. That had been where Tarquin was hiding the first time I'd come up here with Devon—back when the real tower still stood tall in the backdrop of Spellcrest Academy. There had been an open seam, glistening in the center of the room, but Tarquin and his gang of thugs had attacked from the shadows, having already entered our world.

The metallic scent of blood was overpowering, and I fought to push down the rising bile in my throat. As I tore my eyes away from the sickening floor, I noticed feathers floating in the air. I gazed upward and saw more feathers drifting down from the ceiling. I already couldn't remember if they'd been there when I'd first arrived or if they were simply appearing now. However, my question was quickly answered as the room thickened with a deluge of suspended feathers, almost like I was caught in a snowstorm. Suddenly, they were everywhere.

I could no longer see the perimeter of the room through the falling feathers. Neither could I make out the dismembered wings scattered about the floor. Still not willing to move from my spot, I began spinning, not knowing where the attack would come from. I looked for light from an incoming fireball. I searched for any movement behind the downpouring of feathers. My muscles were tensed to the point of straining, anticipating some type of attack from Tarquin. I knew it would be him. Without him, there would be no reason for me to be here.

However, instead of movement capturing my senses, it was a spinetingling voice. "Fly away, little bird. Fly away."

I continued to spin, not being able to pinpoint the direction from where the voice was originating. It was either coming from everywhere or only in my head. I still couldn't see him.

"Let me pluck your wings and send you on your way."

"Where are you, you son of a bitch!" I yelled into the blanket of white.

"I'm right here." An icy cold hand grasped my shoulder from behind and squeezed.

I tried to wrench myself away, but his tightening grip quickly sent me to my knees. Then he set me free. I crumpled to the ground, rolled onto my back, and gazed up into the endless downpouring of feathers, desperately trying to pinpoint my attacker. But he was gone. Swallowed by the feathers currently consuming me.

"Where are you!" I screamed and scrambled to my feet. "Show yourself!"

Suddenly, all the feathers dropped as though they'd crystallized into huge snowflakes and shattered upon impact with the floor. The intense sound of thousands of glasses breaking—the shrill screams of a thousand anguished angels—forced me to cover my ears. And in the next instant, the air was clear, revealing the man I often pictured in my nightmares. Lips sewn shut. Spiders descending from his straggly beard from red thread.

"Hello, little bird," he said as he made his way toward me from across the circular room, crunching through the underbrush of shattered feathers and dismembered wings. "May I have this dance?"

I slowly backed away, cringing from each noisy step, no longer careful to avoid the wings. I soon tripped over one, which crumbled under the sole of my boot.

"This is where we first met," Tarquin said, his voice echoing in my head. His lips did nothing more than twitch. "You were going to cut me free but decided to fly instead. Fly away, little bird."

"Stay back," I warned.

"Or what?" Tarquin continued to splash through the feather crystals, inching his way closer to me.

I backed up at a faster rate but knew a wall was steadily approaching. My only options were fight or fly. I didn't know how transitioning would work in the simulation. It wasn't something I'd done before. Somehow, I didn't think I'd be allowed to leave unless I said the safe word.

Safe house. I wanted to make sure I still remembered it. Saying it in my head didn't trigger the program to act.

Then another hand gripped my shoulder. Tarquin was still visible before me, so someone else had appeared in the room—someone just as impossibly strong.

With all my strength, I threw back an elbow, which collided with something hairy and bony. In pulling away from the loosened grip, I stumbled forward and rolled onto the rocky floor, crunching through more petrified feathers, and caught a glimpse of my new attacker.

Large yellow eyes stared down at me. The

upright form of the wolfman who'd attacked Devon and me in the clearing loomed over me and let out a vicious roar.

I now found myself scrambling in another direction, only to dead end into the monster I'd originally been trying to escape.

"There's my girl," he said and snatched the crystal from my neck, snapping the chain as if it had been crafted from paper. He clasped the crystal in a muscular fist, squeezing it so tightly I thought it might break too and set the soul—*his soul*—free.

The crystal I'd been wearing wasn't any more real than the rest of the simulation since I wasn't allowed to enter the pod while wearing it. But the sight of him clutching the crystal that symbolically held his soul gave me the shivers—the dread that he could somehow find a way to bring himself back to life.

"Stay back, asshole," Tarquin warned, rising to his full height. "This little bird is mine. If you want her, you must come through me."

The werewolf simply snarled, not deterred in the slightest. Then I was seemingly forgotten as the two massive beasts attacked each other. Punches were thrown. Teeth sank into flesh. Bodies were thrown across the stone, shaking the tower so much I was afraid it might collapse with us trapped inside.

I backed up to the nearest wall, on the lookout for any more would-be attackers appearing out of thin air. However, my attention kept returning to the dance of the titans that spanned much of the empty throne room.

I spotted the stairs and considered making a run for it while Tarquin and the werewolf pounded on each other. Neither one seemed guaranteed victory until I climbed to my feet, ready to make a run for it.

Tarquin knocked the wolfman to the ground while clutching tightly to its wrist. The arm twisted and cracked as the beast fell. Tarquin twisted it more, reaching an unnatural angle, then pulled the supernatural canine appendage from its socket with a sickening pop. The arm tore free of its connecting tissue with a splattering of blood.

From the shock of the grotesque sight, I couldn't move. It also didn't help that the fallen wolf was now blocking my path to the stairs. Mental images returned of the angels Tarquin had de-winged in this very tower.

Roars of agony were reduced to whimpers and cries of anguish. By the time he was set aflame, all noise and movement from the werewolf had stopped. His fur helped the fire spread rapidly, reducing him to a blackened mass on the stone floor.

Then Tarquin turned his attention back to me. It was my turn to feel the heat.

"Now, it's time for you to cut me free," he said without the use of his sewn lips. "I'm tired of waiting."

He crunched toward me, still blocking my way to

the stairs. I glanced at the closest window, urgently weighing my options. Ultimately, I decided not to jump. I thought of the confidence my friends had going into today's simulation, as well as how different this interaction had been from the previous ones. The difference had to mean something. My parents were not present in this scenario. This had to symbolize a final showdown with Tarquin—just him and me.

As my bogeyman approached, I attacked first. I shot energy balls from both hands as quickly as I could manifest them. He wouldn't be hurt by them, but I hurled enough magical projectiles his way to throw him off balance. Then I lunged forward, intent on striking as I'd seen Quin do with a seam dagger in Ogginosh. I didn't have a seam dagger, but I had a needle.

While Tarquin continued to block, I called forth my needle. On command, the tip poked through the flesh of my forefinger. I had no intention of pulling it all the way out, but to use it like a mighty claw.

In the moment I stopped firing to retrieve my needle, Tarquin steadied himself and shot back, his magic far more potent than mine. Several fire balls came my way. As much as they burned upon impact, my momentum was too strong to be stopped.

I shouted in pain and determination as my clothes ignited, but by that time I was only a few steps away. Tarquin steadied himself to grab me. I slashed through the air and across his body with my needle claw, opening a seam in midair that extended through his midsection. And unable to stop, I tumbled past him and rolled multiple times over a blanket of crystallized feathers before finally skidding to a stop, also extinguishing the flames from my clothes.

Tarquin couldn't turn to face me, his body impossibly connected to the open seam. I didn't know where it led, and I didn't care. All I cared about was having succeeded in making Tarquin immoveable. He screamed in rage, trying desperately to rotate his body. I remained out of his line of sight as I climbed to my feet, dusting a few remaining embers from my clothes. His upper half thrashed in both directions as he fought to break free of the seam's hold.

"It's no use," I said. "There's nothing you can do." Then I hit him with a fire ball from behind, which really got his attention.

"I will kill you!" he bellowed, sounding as believable as ever. However, he so obviously couldn't back up his words. "Come over to where I can see you!"

I continued to lob fireballs at him, only playing with him now. I sauntered around his planted body with a smug smile plastered across my face.

I did it! I finally beat him!

Still with full usage of his arms, Tarquin produced an energy wave that threw me back against the wall. My head ricocheted off the stone, causing me to drop to a knee before catching myself.

Then I felt an invisible grip on my neck, squeezing until I could barely breathe. I clawed at my throat, but there was nothing tangible to grab hold of. The same invisible force dragged my body forward, toward the unsightly man continuing to stand in two distinct halves.

"I will not let you go until you sew me together again, little bird," Tarquin said, his voice thundering in my head. Within seconds, his face was inches from mine. A spider descending from his beard, landed on my elbow and scurried up my arm, causing me to squeal and shake the creepy critter off my body.

Then the unseen hold on my throat was gone, and I dropped to the floor, coughing and fighting to catch a breath. When I looked back up at Tarquin, he too was gone, replaced by an enveloping void of white.

The class was over. I'd survived.

I may not have killed Tarquin, but I'd survived to the end of class. And I'd gotten close. Perhaps I'd gotten too cocky at the end and let down my guard. I'd had the perfect chance to kill him, but I'd wanted to look him in the eyes first. And the act of pride had prevented me from killing the monster.

But I was close! So damn close!

A part of me wanted to run out of the pod and

insist the SEs put me back into the simulation, allow me to finish what I'd started and correct my foolish mistake. However, that wasn't going to happen. I'd have to wait until tomorrow. And tomorrow I'd be good and goddamned ready.

CHAPTER 17

"*I* did it!" Razielle exclaimed and rushed over when she saw me exit the pod. "I sent that bastard straight to hell!"

"I always knew you could," I said, hugged her, then looked for Erik and Nym.

"What about you?"

"I made definite progress. Not quite the victory you got, but I'm nearly there."

"What did I tell you? Today's the day. We should celebrate."

"I'd love to," I said, grabbing my phone from the locker and slinging my backpack over one shoulder. "But I can't tonight. It seems Devon has made plans for us."

"Ooh, a romantic evening…" Razielle said, mockingly. "Tomorrow night then. I won't take no for an answer."

"Sure thing."

The remainder of our friends joined us outside my pod as more students squeezed by. Erik had a satisfied look on his face, though he wasn't jumping with excitement as Razielle had been. Nym was as even-tempered and unreadable as ever.

"So?" Razielle asked, impatiently.

Erik's face broke into a radiant smile. "Success," he said, smugly.

We all congratulated him before Razielle moved her attention to Nym, but she didn't repeat the question. "Are you okay?" she asked.

"Just peachy," Nym replied, sounding very much like our typically sardonic roommate.

"No worse, right?" I asked, trying to lessen her disappointment to share.

"No better, no worse."

"Then I call this a good news day," I said and wrapped an arm around the vampire elf, who tensed severely at my touch. But she didn't shove me away. I gave her a squeeze then let her go, not wanting to push my luck.

We all went back to our respective rooms to get ready to dinner, though I wouldn't be joining the group at the cafeteria. I was going to meet Devon in the village square for our romantic dinner under the stars—that was, if the clouds dispersed.

And to make the romantic evening complete, I'd be the third wheel because the dinner also included

Clara Long, the Divination TA and Devon's ex-girl-friend. Devon had mentioned us all going out sometime at the beginning of the trimester, but when a few weeks went by without another word about it, I thought I'd dodged the bullet. Perhaps he'd come to his senses, or he wasn't actually serious to begin with. It seemed I was wrong on both counts.

I didn't want to go, but I also didn't want them spending a dinner alone together, either. The test—or attack—on our relationship was still in full effect.

The three of us left the dorm room together. Even though I dreaded my upcoming meal, Nym looked the least excited for dinner.

"Why didn't Devon pick you up like usual?" Razielle asked as we passed through the lounge, the fire in the hearth bright and crackling.

"We just decided to meet at the restaurant," I said with a shrug, as if it was no big deal. I couldn't bring myself to tell her the real reason... not yet.

However, with as skeptical as the Nephilim was, she shot me a look to show she didn't believe me, but she didn't press the issue. I was sure I'd hear about it later, which was good because I'd probably have to vent about the whole stupid situation when I got home.

"Well, enjoy your romantic dinner," Razielle said as we parted ways outside, taking the snow-dusted sidewalk in separate directions.

"You know it," I called over my shoulder while continuing into the brisk, dusk air.

I was jealous of the rest of them, getting to eat a normal, non-awkward dinner—though I supposed those meals didn't apply to Nym anymore, making me feel a little guilty. What were we going to do when she simply couldn't eat regular food anymore?

My pace slowed now that I was on my own. It felt as though I was marching off to some undeserved punishment. So, I was in no hurry to get there. However, when flashes of Devon and Clara together entered my mind, they provided encouragement to reach the village square faster, despite my aversion to this whole engagement.

Spellcrest Village Square was bustling with activity with it being a typical dinner time for many families. Many of the metal tables were already occupied, though it apparently wasn't a problem since Devon and Clara were already here. Clara noticed me, causing Devon to turn and wave me over.

"I hope I didn't keep you guys waiting too long," I said.

"We've only been here a few minutes," Devon said, standing and planting a chaste kiss on my cheek.

Did they arrive together?

"I already put in an order for the three of us at the Italian restaurant. I hope that's okay."

"Sure," I said. *I didn't want Mexican food or anything.* "I take it Miss Long is a big fan of Italian."

"Please, call me Clara, at least while we're not in class," she said, remaining seated. "There aren't any good Italian places nearby back home. We always did love this one, didn't we Devon?"

"We sure did," Devon said with a beaming smile that started with his attention on the white wolf shifter, then made its way to me.

My glare caused his smile to swiftly shrink.

"Clara, you want to save the table while Maeve and I get the food?" Devon asked, and she happily agreed.

I was quiet as we walked to the Italian restaurant on the outskirts of the village square. I distinctly remembered washing the front windows of the small restaurant as one of several punishments when I was a neophyte. And here I was as a sapient, still being punished.

"Is everything okay?" Devon asked as he opened the door for me, and a little bell chimed above our heads.

"Just peachy," I said, channeling my morose vampire roommate.

"I thought it would be good for the two of you to get to know each other. I swear, nothing's going on between us. We're just friends."

"So, this is the restaurant you two used to frequent? You've never taken *me* here."

"I thought it would be weird." Devon approached the to-go counter and requested our food, which was already packaged neatly in brown paper bags, waiting for us.

"Weirder than this?" I asked, though I hadn't spoken loud enough for him to hear.

"You'll like her if you give her a chance," Devon said, passing me one of the bags.

"I'll be nice," I said, which was all I could promise, if I could even promise that.

"Thank you. This really means a lot to me." He picked up the other two bags, looked me deep in the eyes, then leaned in to press his lips against mine.

"Don't think that makes everything better," I scolded him once we parted.

His content smile didn't falter. "It doesn't have to. I just love kissing you."

Okay. That made things slightly better.

We headed back to the table where Clara was waiting and passed out the food. My chicken parmigiana tasted divine, but I made sure to subdue my reaction.

"It's good," I said when asked how my meal was.

"It's just how I remember," Clara said. "I can't believe it's taken me this long to come back here." Her smile faded as she took another few bites, then her demeanor had changed by the time she spoke again. "I should have come back to help out. This school has been through so much since I left. I still can't believe everything you've told me. I mean, not that I don't believe you because I've heard stories from the professors too, but it's just so hard to believe. When has anything like what you guys have been through ever happened here?"

"It hasn't," Devon said, his tone matching hers.

"You left and I arrived," I said. "Either you were protecting the academy with your presence, or I cursed it with mine."

"No, that's something I don't believe," Clara said. "I know a little bit about your family, your mother's family because of Rainley Hall—but you're not cursed."

"Says the bones telling me I'll be attacked."

"Attacked and cursed are not the same thing."

"Was it talking about the attack in the field?" Devon asked. "The werewolf?"

"How the hell should I know?" I said. "Miss Long —I mean Clara is the one who read my fortune in Divination. Even the professor didn't want to admit what it said."

"Well, at least we took care of him."

"Did you though?"

"He's not on campus," Devon said definitively. "Security's keeping a lookout."

"Is it something we should be worried about?" Clara asked.

Devon shook his head. "We don't want to alarm everyone in the school over something so minor.

There are plenty of staff and students with PTSD, still recovering from last year."

"And for good reason," I added.

"I agree, which is why we don't want to start a panic over what's probably nothing."

"Okay," Clara said. "Sounds like you got it covered. I'll leave the security of the school in your capable hands."

"Thank you." Devon gave his ex-girlfriend a warm smile—a prolonged look that went on for way too long.

I didn't have to pretend swallowing my food wrong and broke up the moment by hacking up my lungs.

"Are you okay?" Clara asked, finally prying her hypnotizing eyes away from my boyfriend.

"Fine," I said between lingering coughs, my throat burning. "Just choking."

"I know the Heimlich maneuver."

Of course, you do. "That won't be necessary," I said, regaining my composure and taking a few sips of water. Then I went back to eating what was left on my plate.

The table was quiet for a few minutes while we all focused on eating. Maybe I wasn't the only one who thought this dinner was awkward, just no one else wanted to admit it.

"Maeve, tell me more about you," Clara said to break up the silence. She almost sounded anxious for someone to say something—like Razielle, she apparently didn't do well with long silences.

"What do you want to know?" I asked. "I'm not just going to regale you with my entire life story."

"You came here a few years later than most students, even though your mother's family has a dormitory named after it."

"The headmistress didn't like me," I said, bluntly, glancing at Devon.

Clara laughed and also turned her attention to Devon. "Your mother didn't like me much at the beginning, either."

"That's not true," Devon protested.

Clara eyed him disapprovingly. "It's totally true. She only started warming up to me near the end of our... I don't think she likes anyone initially. Do you remember the first thing your mother said to me?"

"I can't say that I do."

"'Do you color your hair?' she'd asked. When I told her I didn't—that my hair was naturally white— she suggested I should." Clara laughed, but it was a forced, strained laugh that suggested the exchange with the headmistress still bothered her.

"That's pretty awful," I said. "But at least she didn't try to actively keep you from coming here. I knew nothing about my mother's legacy here when I started. My brother and I came into this place knowing jack shit abut magic."

"And here you are, the next powerful seamstress."

"My needle practically forced Headmistress Christi to take me in. But she despised me from day one."

"No arguments here," Devon said, when Clara looked his way for confirmation of my comment. "I'll admit she wasn't your biggest fan, but she's grown to like you more than I could have hoped for."

"Is this true?" Clara asked, turning back to me.

"Yeah, she's weirdly nice to me now," I said, twirling the last of my noodles around my fork. "I still can't explain that one. She must've done some heavy soul searching while she was dead."

"Okay, so how did you get here?"

Clara was really pushing for a story, so I gave in and gave her the abridged version. I left out minor details such as my brother stealing my needle and not getting it back until Tarquin was killed, the soul of whom I now wore around my neck.

My hand reflexively rose to my chest at the thought of my soul crystal—only to find it wasn't there. I patted my chest several times, convinced I simply missed it. However, the reality that I didn't have my crystal quickly kicked in.

How could I have not noticed its absence earlier?

I'd had it on earlier in the day, just never going a whole day without wearing it.

So, the only logical thing I could think of was having forgotten it at Combative Casting—in the small locker where I stowed my phone.

I jumped out of my seat before I'd even finished my story. "I'm sorry, but I have to go."

"Really, now?" Devon asked, his voice laced with concern. "We barely sat down."

"I just remembered a bunch of homework I forgot was due tomorrow," I lied, not very convincingly.

"Just stay like another twenty minutes. You'll still have plenty of time to finish whatever homework you—"

"No, I have to go now."

"Then I'll come with you. Walk you back to the dorm."

"No," I protested. "Finish your food. Don't worry about me. Finish catching up and whatnot." And before any more arguments could be made, I picked up my trash, gave Devon a long, possessive kiss, and proceeded to the nearest trashcan.

I'd been looking for an excuse to escape the awkward dinner from hell, and as soon as one presented itself, I took full advantage. However, this was also not just *some* excuse. I couldn't afford to lose my soul crystal. It was as significant as leaving behind my phone or wallet—maybe even more so. And if it wasn't in my locker, then I didn't know what I'd do.

CHAPTER 18

From the trashcan, I glanced back at the table from which I'd left Devon and Clara and found them still watching me. At least their conversation for the next few minutes would be centered around me instead of their old relationship. I didn't initially consider that a bad thing, but guessed it could be interpreted as such.

Let's talk about your crazy girlfriend running off like a loon in the night.

I didn't want to think about where *that* conversation would lead.

Nowhere good, I supposed.

Before I made it out of the village square, I noticed a hooded figure sitting alone at one of the far tables, immediately reminding me of the creepy watcher from earlier in the trimester, the one I'd tried to point out to Devon.

Unfortunately, he had disappeared before Devon could see who I was pointing out.

And here he was again—assuming it was a man. In the dark, I couldn't see through the shadows created by the hood. At first, it seemed as though he was watching me leave the village square, but once my attention turned in his direction, his shifted elsewhere.

Was he now focused on Devon and Clara? It was the instant connection I made, but I couldn't tell. Too many tables were stationed around the square to be sure.

I could have been blowing the whole damn thing out of proportion.

Paranoia from other areas of the evening could have been bleeding into my current judgment and making me see things that weren't there, making me see ghosts.

I considered going back to the table to point him out to Devon or marching up to the hooded guy's table and asking him what the hell he was doing. However, I was quickly reminded of why I'd jumped up from the table to begin with, continuing my current quest.

Just because someone was looking in my general direction didn't mean he was watching me. Just because someone was sitting at a table with his hood pulled up in the evening—in the middle of winter—

didn't make him suspicious. I was creating these stories in my mind. All the trauma I'd been through was warping my thinking, something I needed to start recognizing.

I continued scolding myself as I rushed to Shadow Peaks Hall on the far side of the campus, past all the other dormitories. Its backdrop showcased the severe angles of the Manor, now the tallest building without the lonely tower. The headmistress's office, located at the top of the tallest turret, shone brightly in the darkened, starlit sky.

Making a hard turn before the Manor, I passed the cafeteria before reaching the sapient dormitory. I followed a few other students inside, giving brief pleasantries as I passed, though refusing to slow my pace.

Students had no reason to visit the basement after hours, so my echoing footfalls were the only sound as I marched in the direction of the highly specialized Combative Casting classroom. I expected the door to be locked, not that it would keep me out.

My needle thought nothing of locked doors.

However, my seamstress abilities were not required to get into the training room. The door was unlocked, and the lights were on.

"Hello? Is anyone here?" I called into the large, empty room as I gently assisted the door in closing.

When there was no answer, and I didn't see

anyone at the SE station, I made a beeline for the row of pods. With my heart pounding, I opened the door to my locker and reached inside. My hand felt around, then came away empty.

Shit.

I bent down and peered inside.

And there was my crystal necklace, pushed to the back of the locker.

With a flood of relief, I grabbed and hung it around my neck, immediately feeling the warmth I hadn't noticed I'd been missing.

The familiar rage of my crystallized passenger gave me the satisfaction that I was still in control, and it made me smile.

You can't get rid of me that easily, you miserable son of a bitch.

We're connected, you and I.

"Maeve? What are you doing here?"

I spun around at the sound of the vaguely familiar voice, only to find one of the simulation engineers staring at me.

I gasped as a hand jumped to my chest, this time feeling the crystal I'd been missing earlier. "What are you trying to do to me?"

"Sorry. I didn't mean to scare you," Elliott the SE said. He was only a few inches taller than me, with black-rimmed classes and equally dark, wavy hair. "But I wasn't expecting anyone in here after Professor Ocumulus left."

"I announced myself when I arrived," I said, taking a few breaths to calm down. My paranoia really was getting to me. I'd never been this jumpy before.

"I had earbuds in. I guess I didn't hear you." He nervously glanced around, as if he was expecting to find someone else in the room. "What are you doing here?"

"I forgot something in my locker. I didn't expect to find anyone still in here, either."

"I was just closing up. The simulations are all updated and ready for tomorrow."

"*Fantastic*," I said, sarcastically. "Got to make sure they're in tiptop shape to torture us."

Elliott didn't look amused. "They're not torture devices. They're—"

"Training devices. We've been told."

"You're the seamstress, right?" Elliott's eyes lowered slightly, glancing at my chest—which was becoming something far too common.

"Did the big tattoo on my chest give it away?" I placed my hands on my hips and glowered at him.

"I wasn't looking—I mean, I read it in your file—I just hadn't actually talked to you this year, unless you count my introduction to the whole class."

"I don't. And it's fine." I'd had enough awkwardness for one night. No need to make things worse. I used to revel in interactions like these, but now was just starting to feel bad.

"It's so interesting having a seamstress using the simulator. You really test all the parameters and algorithms we have in place. It'll be a giant leap forward for us."

"*Yay*. Always glad to help," I said, already starting to back away into the open part of the classroom. "I'll get out of your hair."

"Are you interested in participating in another simulation?" he asked, attempting to keep me from leaving.

"That's quite alright. One simulation a day is more than enough."

"Well, if you ever do, I can arrange it. Any night you want. The professor won't mind."

"Thanks, but no thanks."

As Elliott tried to think of something more compelling to make me stay, I rushed out of the room. At the risk of sounding conceited, I didn't need another guy drooling over me. This was the first time he'd officially talked to me, and after tonight, I feared it wouldn't be the last.

Once I was out of there, I let relief wash over me and let out a long sigh. I was whole again. The awkwardness of the night was over. I did have some homework to do, but nothing that needed to be turned in tomorrow, so I planned to take the rest of the night off. I freakin' deserved it.

I headed back to our dorm room, hoping the girls

would be there. I needed to vent about the ridiculousness of the evening. The hallway was empty, though I could hear talking and music coming from various rooms I passed.

As I drew closer to our room, I started to notice something wasn't right. Blood red letters were scrawled across one of the doors, which I soon realized was ours. I stopped dead before our door, unable to breathe as I read the message in my head.

Go home, bloodsucker.

I couldn't believe what I was reading—that someone would do this. Nym had been going through enough... and now to deal with this?

I scanned both sides of the hallway. Still empty. No doors opening or closing. No hallway cameras to record whoever did this.

The letters were thick, more substantial than having been written in marker. Some had drip marks connecting one word to another, others traveling halfway down the door.

Shit.

I touched the lettering and found it dry. Nothing rubbed off onto my finger. I tried scrubbing it with my middle finger. The paint—or whatever the words had been written in—refused to smear.

Double shit. I needed to get this message off before Nym saw it and went ballistic.

I brought my ear closer to the door to listen for

any noise inside, and just as I thought I heard some-one, the door swung inward and an incredulous Razielle was staring at me.

"What are you doing out here?" she asked, holding the door open.

CHAPTER 19

*B*efore Razielle had a chance to notice what was written on the door, I pulled her ass into the hallway. From the moment she'd opened up, I'd noticed Nym at her desk in the background. This was not going to be easy.

"What the hell, Maeve!" Razielle exclaimed.

"Keep your voice down," I said between gritted teeth. I didn't know if we could manage a conversation without Nym overhearing, but we had to try. Then without saying another word, I placed my hands on Razielle's face and forced her to turn around.

When she cried out in shock, I clasped a hand over her mouth to keep her quiet—never an easy task with the Nephilim.

"Okay, so you haven't seen this already," I whispered. "And with that, I'll assume Nym hasn't, either."

"Did you see anyone?" she asked.

I grabbed her arm and pulled her away from our door, not stopping until we were about five doors away. "No," I finally answered. "How is it you heard me standing outside, but you didn't hear someone tagging our door?"

"Nym heard you."

"That's exactly my point. How didn't she hear the asshole—*or assholes*—defacing our property?"

Razielle shrugged. "I dunno. They must have been quieter than you. I guess you should work on that."

"This coming from *you*—perhaps the loudest person I know."

"You asked, and we're not talking about me." Razielle walked to the opposite side of the hallway for a better view of our vandalized door. "What are we gonna do? Nym could open the door at any moment, wondering what we're doing out here. She probably thinks we're plotting against her."

"Which is why she's probably listening for information, but will remain inside—at least for now," I said. "So, we need to act fast. We need to clean the door without her knowing anything's wrong."

"Know any good cleaning spells?"

I shook my head. "It really should be taught in one of our classes."

"I think it is in Advanced Evo. We just haven't gotten to it yet."

"Well, that doesn't help." I took a few moments staring at the door to think. "Here's what we'll do. You go back into the room, act as if everything's fine, and keep Nym in there. In the meantime, I'll enlist help to get our door cleaned up."

"I should be able to manage that for the next hour or so," Razielle said. "After that, she'll want to wash up for bed. It's not like I can tell her *no*. I don't even know if I can physically stop her at this point. She's getting stronger by the day."

"I know—I've got a time crunch. I can get it done before then," I said. I'd have to. I had no other choice.

With a nod of agreement, Razielle headed back to the room. I waited until she was inside to make sure there weren't any immediate complications before seeking the help I required.

Since cutting a seam wasn't an option, I focused on transitioning. Since I'd recently left Devon and Clara in the village square, I could vividly picture the surroundings, the table where we were sitting, and the arrangement of those left at the table.

I closed my eyes and pictured myself back in the chair I'd vacated. At the last moment, with the newly formulated fear of ending up on someone's lap, I pictured myself appearing behind Devon instead.

I focused intensely on the spot in which I wanted to appear. The warmth of the dormitory hallway faded, and I felt a cold blast of the winter night air. Then a gasp, as I apparently startled the couple left at the table we'd been sharing not too long ago.

I opened my eyes just in time to see Clara pull her hand away from Devon's, which remained precariously in place on the metal grate table.

"Maeve…" Devon said, his eyes wide, no other words seemingly able to escape his lips.

I didn't know where to place my growing hurt, betrayal, and indignation. I had come to Devon for help, and suddenly, I couldn't stand the sight of him.

And Clara… She appeared to be a problem from the moment she got here.

First, it was Razielle afraid she'd steal Ivanic away. Then I'd found out she was Devon's ex-girlfriend, so the doubt crept into my life and relationship.

I'd never been good at bottling up my emotions.

Neither had I been good at rationally expressing my emotions in a fit of rage. I always ended up hurting someone—emotionally, physically, or both.

While I struggled to remember why I'd returned in the first place, I curled my right hand into a fist, my death glare aimed at Devon. But at the last second, I spun my attention and my aim, launching a non-magical fist right at Clara's stunned face.

Not expecting the power of my punch, her head whipped backward, her back slamming into the chair. During the moments it took her to process what had happened, blood began gushing from her potentially broken nose.

The burn in my hand from the impact brought me back to the present and realization of what I'd done.

No one moved. Clara didn't cry out, though she quickly cupped her bleeding nose. Everyone—including me—was stunned.

Just when I thought I'd outgrown the impulsive side of myself, something bad enough had to happen to drag me back down. My defense mechanism for retaining control of the situation. Though was I really? Did this make me in control?

"Maeve…" Devon was still having a hard time speaking, even though he wasn't the one with blood pouring over his lips.

I stretched my burning hand, then formed another fist.

"It's not what it looks like," he apprehensively continued. "Nothing happened—or was going to happen. You have to believe—"

But I was gone before hearing the rest of his sentence. I immediately teleported back to the dormitory hallway just as the emotional response of what I'd witnessed and done hit me in the chest with a sledgehammer.

Unable to breathe, but not willing to cry, I gazed upon the grotesque graffiti covering our door and realized what I'd failed to do. I'd gone to enlist help and returned empty handed.

I needed to think of someone new, but my mind was no longer functioning properly. I didn't know what to do next.

Mom. She can help.

However, as soon as the thought appeared, our dorm room door opened, and I saw the side of Nym's head as she digested the message while Razielle yelled from inside the room.

My new problem quickly became white noise as concern rose for my emotionally fragile friend.

"Nym, don't—don't read it!" I yelled and rushed down the hallway to force her back into the room. My rational side already knew it was too late, but my emotional side couldn't stop fighting to protect her. And my emotional side primarily won.

I tried to push her into the room, allow the door to close, and make the awful message disappear, but she wouldn't budge. Razielle was right with how strong Nym had become. I pushed and Razielle pulled on one arm, but Nym remained impossibly anchored to her spot before the open door. She showed no emotion, just staring endlessly at the words scrawled across the door.

Finally, I gave up. I stopped pushing. Razielle soon followed my lead and did the same, allowing Nym's arm to drop.

I didn't know the right thing to say. Perhaps

there wasn't a right thing to say. "We didn't want you to see this—to have to see this," I said, stumbling over the words. "I'm sorry."

"Me too," Razielle added.

Nym didn't immediately respond. "I have no home. No one wants me here. No one wants me in the place I used to call home. I don't belong anywhere."

"That's not true." I leaned in to hug her, but she pushed me away before I could lock my arms around her—and her emerging vampire strength sent me sprawling to the floor.

She looked at me in horror, still unsure of her own strength.

I threw my hands up in a peaceful gesture. "It's okay. I'm okay. I understand you're upset."

"I'm a monster!" she cried, pointing to the words on the door. "And this proves it! All of this!"

"That's not true!" I fired back, but she was retreating as fast as I had with Devon.

She bolted down the hallway, down the stairs, and out of sight within seconds—moving as fast as anyone could without teleporting.

My attention returned to Razielle, still holding the door open with one foot.

She was chewing on her lower lip and shaking her head.

"Well, that sucked," she said once the initial shock wore off. "What are we gonna do now?"

"You ask me like I have all the answers," I said.

"Which is something we've all come to expect. Who's coming to fix the door?"

Now, it was my turn to shake my head. "No one yet. Where do you think the little elf will go?"

"I wish I knew that too." Razielle's voice was quiet and sullen, turning to match her dark wardrobe style. "I don't expect her to answer texts right now."

I suspected she was right, but it wasn't good for her to be alone right now. It wasn't safe for her to be in such an emotional state with the control—or lack thereof—she currently commanded on her changing abilities.

I messaged Mom about the emergency, and she came to our aid in a flash, along with Guy and Quin. One look at our dorm room door and Mom nearly went on a swearing tirade. I didn't know she had it in her, but understood this was personal for her too from her own roommate experience.

The infamous Dawn Carmichael.

By the end of last year's disaster, I had come to understand Dawn wasn't the bad guy, but it was still hard to get past all the awful things she had done even though supposedly under the influence of the plague vampires.

"This is the kind of prejudice Kicryria aims to rid this world of," Guy said as Mom magically erased the inexcusable message from our door.

"And the magical elite of Earth paint *us* as the problem."

"Do you have any ideas as to who did this?" Quin asked.

"Not at all," Razielle said, passing around our section of the hallway. "I'm gonna start looking. I can't wait any longer."

"We should split up," I said. "We'll be able to cover more ground."

"I'll talk with some of the staff tomorrow," Mom said once the door was clean. "See if any of them have overheard students mentioning or discussing anything retaliatory toward vampires."

"Some of the staff might be the problem. You saw what they put up in Memorial Hall. And it's still there. What will it take to make them do something?"

"I've talked to the headmistress, as have you. It'll get fixed. It just takes time."

"Time we don't have," I argued and pointed to the door. "Time leads to shit like this."

"I know." Mom sounded sympathetic, but she didn't backtrack her statement.

"*We* can retaliate," Quin suggested. However, Mom immediately shut such a notion down.

"We're wasting more time," Razielle said, continuing to pace like a caged tiger. "Since I'm the only one who can fly, I'll start scanning the area from the sky and let you know what I find."

We all agreed that would be the best use of her abilities, so Razielle took off while the rest of us decided on the best way to break up the campus.

"Where would Nym feel safest?" Mom asked.

"I don't know," I admitted. "She doesn't feel safe anywhere anymore. I'll start with contacting the rest of our group, though I doubt she simply went a friend's room."

"What about her boyfriend?" Guy asked. "The guy with the GQ hair. What's his name?"

"Toby. He already graduated and is attending university... I can't remember where."

"Family?" Quin asked.

"All on the East Coast," I said. "And they're not her biggest fan right now."

"An unsupportive family makes the transition so much harder than it needs to be," Mom said.

I couldn't agree more, but that wasn't an obstacle we were going to tackle today. Not wanting to prolong the discussion, we settled on sections of the campus we were each going to cover.

Mom headed toward the Manor. Guy took the west. Quin took the east.

And I headed toward Windsor Hall after contacting Ivanic.

I gave him the task of messaging the rest of the group to ensure Nym hadn't gone to them for sanctuary. Then Ivanic insisted on meeting up with me to help search. I didn't slow down for him, but he quickly caught up. By the time I had passed the cafeteria, he'd come running up from behind me. He wasn't even breathing heavy when he skidded to a stop beside me, leaving a long mark in the dusting of snow on the sidewalk.

I told Ivanic about his girlfriend scanning the school from the air, and as we continued down the sidewalk, we periodically looked upward to see if either of us could spot her.

"There," Ivanic said, pointing into the distance. "Beyond the wall."

At first glance, I thought he was pointing out a bird. The flying figure looked too small to be our sardonic Nephilim. However, I used the academy wall as a reference point and realized how deceptive her size was from this distance.

"She's really out there," I said.

"She can cover a lot of ground quickly."

I didn't know how well she could see from so high up in the dark, but had faith in my friend.

We stopped in the lobby of Windsor Hall, with its great open space, candlelit chandelier towering overhead, and the grand curved staircase. I couldn't remember the last time I'd been in this building, but memories of first arriving at Spellcrest with Finley and Otis flooded my head. I could still see Professor Windsor descending the staircase, coming to greet us. And her taking me to the third floor to meet the roommates I now regarded as my best friends and sisters. It was the first time Finley and I would spend apart… and we'd been apart ever since.

"Should we start knocking on doors?" Ivanic asked, pulling me from my reverie.

"I don't see that as productive," I said. "Though checking out the basement classrooms might not be a bad idea."

We headed toward one classroom in particular, which held special meaning for the entire group of us sapients. The classroom where we'd all become friends—where I had met Devon. There were times in this classroom when I'd hated him, and times when I'd loved him.

I'd even made love to him for the first time in this very classroom, which I wasn't about to admit to anyone else in the group—especially the boy I was currently with.

However, the thought of Devon now simply infuriated me. We'd experienced so many trust issues early on, and here we were, right back where we'd started.

Ivanic and I ventured into the classroom, and flipped on the lights.

I didn't even need my needle to bypass the locked door.

My skills with turning a lock from the inside had only gotten better over time.

I took a deep breath, frustrated by the conflicting memories muddling my mind. I had to put aside the anger and resentment for my relationship situation to focus all my energy on helping Nym. And with one good look around, it was obvious she wasn't here. We needed to move on.

Ivanic and I took opposite sides of the hallway to get through the basement classrooms quickly. Since Nym wasn't in the classroom that held meaning for our group, I didn't have high hopes of finding her in one of the others. But I wasn't about to leave without at least a cursory look.

"Any luck?" Ivanic asked as we reached the stairs again, after circling the basement.

"If I had, then you'd know," I said.

By this point, he knew not to take my sarcasm too personally. It came out even more than usual under times of stress.

Once we were back out in the nighttime air, I glanced around the open grounds at the snow-covered topiaries and sporadically placed benches. The few occupied benches I found did not reveal a hiding elf.

Ivanic was searching the sky again, but now there was no Razielle to be seen. Her circle must have widened well past the academy wall. I didn't imagine Nym taking off into the forest, but she wasn't the girl she used to be, and I could hardly imagine what she was capable of now.

"Where to now?" Ivanic asked as his attention returned to Earth.

"We're almost to the village, so I say we continue in this direction," I said.

"She doesn't go the village very often."

"Which is precisely why she might not think anyone would look for her there. We have others checking other parts of the campus. Spellcrest Village widens our search area."

Ivanic agreed on our next destination, so we marched toward the main gate.

The village square was emptier than when I'd left it the second time. Devon had yet to reach out to me, though I was sure he was giving me time to calm down.

Adequate space was an important part of our relationship.

Apart from scanning the open area of tables and shops, I specifically searched out the table where we'd been sitting. It was now empty, with several trash items left behind. That added to my irritation.

"You look like you want to hit somebody," Ivanic commented, at which point I noticed him standing just out of striking range.

"Before the shit happened with Nym, I got into it with Devon," I said, and reflexively, my hands balled into fists again.

"Sorry. Sounds like you're not having the best night."

"It could have gone better. I could have handled it better. I could do a lot of things differently."

"What happened with you and Devon?" Ivanic asked.

"Remember your favorite wolf shifter TA?" I said, keeping the sarcasm thick and heavy. I started walking again, weaving slowly through the tables.

"I'm not allowed to talk about her anymore." He sounded serious.

"You know she's Devon's ex, right?" I asked. When Ivanic nodded, I continued. "I witnessed something—lingering feelings? Unresolved feelings? I dunno. Despite Devon's promise that there's nothing left between them, there is. I saw it—and I lost it. I might have punched her in the face."

"You punched our TA?" Ivanic went from disbelief to laughter in the span of two seconds.

"I'm not proud of it." My gaze continued to scan the tables and open space around the perimeter of the square. The guy with the hood who'd creeped me out earlier was also gone.

That's a universal truth about creepers, they're always on the move.

"Do you think she'll keep TAing in Divination?" Ivanic asked.

"If I weren't so cursed, I'd let myself dream of her transferring to somewhere else. I'm confident I'm not that lucky."

As we continued through the village square with no clear sign of Nym, my phone buzzed in my back pocket. When I took it out, Razielle's name was flashing across the screen.

"You better have some good news," I said, answering the call.

"I found her," Razielle said.

CHAPTER 20

azielle was calling from the air, and I warned her about dropping her phone —*again*. The erratic Nephilim assured me she was in complete control.

I've heard that before.

Razielle had spotted Nym outside the academy wall.

The forest wasn't a safe place for any of us students after dark, so I wanted to get to her quickly and coax her back within range of the academy protection spell. I texted Mom about our success and Ivanic texted the rest of our friends, to prevent needless worry.

We hurried farther into the village, cutting through a townhome yard near the turn of the academy wall. There were no other footprints in the snow, so I didn't know if Nym had gone this way or if her prints had since been covered by magical or nonmagical means.

We trekked between the high wall and tree line, the same way I used to take to reach the lonely tower. Now, no such monolith dominated the backdrop.

Where the tower once stood had been reduced to a chaotic mountain of stones. And there was our friend, sitting amidst the rubble.

Nym was alone, Razielle not wanting to approach her on her own. I suspected Nym saw Ivanic and me coming, but she didn't signal that she did. She remained still on her crumbling throne.

As we drew close, Razielle swooped to touch down beside us, so we could all carefully confront the little elf together.

"What made you choose this place?" I asked, reaching the edge of the stone pile and gazing up to where Nym was seated.

"It's all that's left of my birthplace," Nym responded, gazing out at the dark horizon instead of down at us. "Those monsters made me into what I've become—another monster. As much as I hate them, my fate is now tied to them. I don't have anyone else to turn to."

"You have us," I said. "We're here for you with whatever you need."

"I need someone who understands me. I'm sorry,

but you don't. You have no idea what I'm going through."

"Maybe not exactly, but I know plenty about being an outsider. I grew up feeling different and not accepted by anyone else, and I learned not to let others' opinions of me dictate how I thought about myself." I stopped, hoping she'd finally look at me. She didn't, but I kept going regardless. "Despite what you may think, you're not a monster. You need to stop thinking about yourself that way. You'll become your own worst enemy."

Nym still didn't respond.

I gauged the precarious grouping of rocks to determine my best way to reach her. I tested a few at the bottom to see if they moved. One did, so I avoided it and chose another. I wasn't graceful as I ascended the rock pile, but was determined. Despite a few slips and missteps, I kept climbing.

Razielle spread her gorgeous ivory wings and bypassed the climb completely. She carefully set herself down on the opposite side of Nym from where I was attempting to locate a stable seat.

When I slipped again and the rocks beneath me began to slide, a strong hand gripped my upper arm and kept me from tumbling to the ground. Nym would never have been able to hold me up with one hand in her former life, but was doing it with ease now.

"Don't let go," I urged, scrambling to reclaim

stable footing.

"I've got you," Nym said.

"Do you need any help?" Razielle asked, trying to reach past Nym, but not being successful without moving to a new spot on the rocks.

"I'm ready too," Ivanic said from the ground, positioning himself under me.

We were a powerful team. No one could deny that. And I wasn't the self-proclaimed leader anymore. We didn't have a leader. We didn't need one. We all led when necessary, and we all stepped aside when it was time for someone else to take the reins.

"I won't let you fall," Nym said, continuing to keep me steady.

Another rock under one foot fell away, but my other foot found a secure one. I eased pressure onto the steady rock until it held my entire weight. Then I could choose my next stable step. After a few more maneuvers, I found my seat next to Nym, and she hesitantly let go of my arm.

"See? Piece of cake," I said with a sheepish smile.

"Yeah, you really showed us how it's done," Ivanic said. "I'll be sure to follow your path."

I turned to Nym, wanting to bring the focus back on her. "What you did for me was amazing. Do you realize that? Can you honestly say you could've done it before?"

"I am a little bit stronger now," Nym said, shyly.

"A little bit? You're not a monster, you're a freakin' superhero!"

The others agreed—well, everyone besides Nym.

"Look at the positives with your new abilities. You're so focused on the negatives. But look at you— you're absolutely amazing."

"I'll always want you on my team," Razielle said. "Best friends forever. The three amigas."

"The three amigas," I seconded. I put an arm around our little elf's shoulder, daring her to throw me off again. Nym stiffened, but didn't pull away. And when she saw it was safe, Razielle joined in, wrapping an arm around our friend from the opposite side.

"Will you come back to the room now?" I asked. "The writing is gone. It's all taken care of."

"Can I have a while longer—alone?" Nym asked. "You know where I am now; I'm not running away. I just need to finish clearing my head."

"I respect your personal space and desire to be alone, but I can't in good conscience leave you— superhero or not. There are real monsters out here. We should all be inside the wall." I released her from my side of the hug. "But we don't have to leave right away, if you don't want."

When I glanced back to Ivanic, I noticed a pile of clothes and a restless cougar in his place. His cougar form paced at the base of the rock mountain, his attention focused on the nearby line of trees—the dark forest where the nocturnal predators lurked. He now fit right in.

"It's dangerous for Spellcrest students to be venturing out into the night," a voice proclaimed.

The voice wasn't familiar, and it took me a moment to find where it was coming from.

A figure seemed to emerge from the academy wall and stepped into the open clearing between the wall, rocks, and trees. The male figure wore all black, with a hood pulled up, making him appear faceless in the moonlit darkness.

It's the guy from the village.

I'd thought he'd been watching me, but I'd convinced myself I was being paranoid and didn't do anything to raise an alarm. Well, an alarm was raised now.

"I've seen you before," I said, wanting to stand, but afraid the movement would send me tumbling forward—not exactly a sign of strength. "You were in the village. Why the hell are you following me?"

"Why are you children outside the safety of the academy?" the mysterious man countered.

There was a strange energy to the man that I couldn't quite place. I was drawn to him—in a way I'd never felt before, a magical pull that set my chest on fire.

I couldn't tell if it was my crystal or the octagram tattoo, but at least one of them was on high alert. My hands were tingling with radiant energy.

The cougar form of Ivanic growled at the intruder, lowering his head, and advancing slowly. The man did not appear afraid of the approaching cougar, watching him, but holding his ground.

"I'd keep my distance if I were you, little kitty," the man said, almost sounding playful. "You may bite, but I bite harder."

"Ivanic, don't," I warned, not knowing what this man was capable of. He certainly didn't look intimidated, which was usually a cause for concern.

But as usual, Ivanic didn't listen when it came to protecting his friends. He roared and snapped at the man, attempting to force him back a few steps, but still failing to intimidate him.

I'd seen how this cougar could tear an opponent wide open, exposing innards and gore. I'd seen how quickly the supernatural beast could move. But even with the vicious predator only a dozen feet away from the man in black, he still looked completely relaxed.

Suddenly, Ivanic the cougar lunged at the man with a mighty roar, but he was knocked aside in midair by an impenetrable force that sent him flying with a burst of lime green light. The roar morphed into a scream of pain as the cougar hit the ground and rolled through the snow.

"Ivanic!" Razielle screamed, extended her wings, launching herself off the rock mountain. Her sudden movement caused a shift under the rest of us.

"No! Razielle!" I yelled after her, and with a simple shift of my weight, started sliding down what quickly became a small avalanche of rocks. I was swept up in the flood and rocks collided with me from above as I continued to fall.

I didn't come close to landing on my feet, crashing onto the ground with rocks raining around me, battering me left and right. Being pummeled was just as bad as an onslaught of magical fireballs, with bruises instead of burns marring my body. And just when I thought I'd hit rock bottom, my right hand slid between two stones, then a final tumbling boulder slammed right on top of my wrist and forced it to an angle it was never meant to go. A snap louder than the colliding rocks rang out, and I screamed at the sharp pain that followed.

My friends were still fighting the mysterious man in black, but stars appeared in my vision, and my darkened surrounding began to steadily lose more of its clarity.

A fireball flash brighter than the stars in my vision caught my attention. It had come from Razielle hovering a few feet above the man, casting her hellfire upon him. She put everything into her attack, but he easily absorbed the energy. One of her flapping wings swung too close, allowing the man to grab a handful of feathers and launch her toward a partially recovered Ivanic.

I pictured the dismembered angel wings littering

the lonely tower floor in my recent simulation, hoping to God that wasn't a premonition of tonight's fight.

Suddenly, Nym was at my side and lifted the boulder from my wrist. I was able to pull my hand free, but any movement of my right arm sent lightning bolts past my shoulder. I cradled my injured arm, managing to sit upright.

Nym gave me a sympathetic nod before turning and facing the man in black.

A low growl sounded deep in her throat, a rumble as vicious and animalistic as Ivanic's in his cougar form. Nym remained between our attacker and me, doing her best to keep me out of harm's way in my compromised state.

Healing abilities would come in handy right about now, but it seemed to be a gap in the academy curriculum thus far. I guessed they were saving it for the Master Classmen.

Nym shot several energy balls at the man in black before lunging for him with full force. She wasn't Dawn fast, but so much faster than she used to be—or the rest of us were. However, her opponent was not another student. The man in black deflected her energy balls and readied himself for her attack. He blocked her first blow, pivoted to the side, and used her momentum against her to send her tumbling to the snow-covered ground.

Nym rolled several times before jumping back to

her feet, relatively unfazed. She took stock of her surroundings before rushing in for another attack. Ivanic the cougar and Razielle were also recovered and closing in on the man from multiple directions.

"The academy is training you well," the man said, glancing around the circle he was now in the middle of. "But you must understand you still lack critical experience. Simulations, as effective as they are, cannot replace the real thing."

I was intrigued by the man's words. He obviously had Spellcrest experience, most likely, a former student. Since I'd never got a good look at his face, I had no idea how old he was—or how old he appeared since looks could be deceiving.

"Well, if you knew anything about the past few years, then you'd know many of us have had real-life experience," Razielle said. "Killing people in a simulation *is* different than killing someone in real life. And all of us here have done both. So, don't placate us like your garden-variety students.

"Who the hell are you and what do you want?"

"Just her," the man said and pointed to me. Then he disappeared from the center of the circle. In the next instant, he was standing before me, having completely bypassed my defending friends. "Time to go, seamstress." He reached for my injured arm, and the fear of not being able to fight him off consumed me.

CHAPTER 21

*B*efore the man in black was able to lay a finger on me, Nym collided into him, and they both spilled onto the rock mountain.

Nym landed on top of him, flashed her fangs, and sank them into his neck. The man in black struggled for release, but Nym clung tightly to him with every available appendage to keep from being thrown off. He tried to push her head away, but her teeth were securely in his flesh, ready to rip out his throat if enough force was supplied.

The man stopped struggling to pry the vampire off his body, then placed both hands on her waist. As his hands started to glow bright orange, Nym's clothes burst into flames. She released her fangs to scream, and her preoccupation on the pain gave the man the opportunity to throw her backwards with a magical tidal wave.

He placed one hand on his bleeding neck and pushed off the incline of rocks. In the struggle, his hood had slid off, revealing a glimpse of his face in the dim moonlight.

I'd expected to discover this man was someone I recognized, shocked to realize I hadn't suspected him of wanting me for some nefarious reason. But I didn't recognize him at all. I'd never seen the man before in my life.

What the hell does this guy want with me?

However, it seemed he'd momentarily forgotten about me. Nym's attack on him had struck a nerve, and he wanted revenge.

After rolling several rotations in the snow, Nym had put out the flames threatening to consume her clothes. Steam still rose from where the snow had battled the fire and won.

Nym knew she was in trouble and climbed back to her feet. Razielle and Ivanic the cougar were also ready for the man in black as they stalked toward Nym.

We were in trouble. It was a mistake to always think we could take care of things on our own. Yes, we had experience. But even experienced fighters got themselves in over their heads. It was clear to me now that this guy was dangerous.

I awkwardly fished the phone out of my pocket with my left hand, resting my broken right arm on my leg. But my arm still moved. I was forced to twist my body to reach my phone, which hurt like hell.

The man in black caught Nym in some invisible hold, hurling more fireballs her way.

Ivanic leaped at him from one side, and as soon as the man batted him away, Razielle hit him from the other.

I maneuvered to unlock my phone, realizing how helpful that ambidextrous tattoo I'd intended to get last year would have helped right now.

But before I was able to make a call, I noticed a blue light slice through the air.

A tip of a knife blade emerged from it, arcing down and opening a seam twenty feet away.

Then Quin stepped out of the void, followed by Mom and Guy.

They each surveyed the scene, noticed the immediate threat with the man in black and rushing to aid my friends. He was now encircled six to one, and as he assessed his odds, he must also have realized he'd be fighting more than *inexperienced* students.

The man in black donned his hood, shot one more glance my way, then disappeared into the nighttime void.

My mother had questions for those who'd been fighting the mysterious man, then proceeded to heal any lingering injuries.

Guy was the first to make his way over to me. "It's not like you to sit out a fight, firecracker," he said before noticing me cradling my arm. "Need some help with that?"

"If you don't mind," I said. "I heard it break, and it hurts like a bitch."

"If it kept you out of the scuffle, then I'd bet it does." Guy squatted before me, carefully enclosing my wrist with two icy hands.

Within seconds, my entire arm felt as if encased in ice and quickly went numb.

Guy didn't pry his eyes from mine as he worked, gazing at me seeming to provide all the concentration he needed.

"Are you okay?" a concerned voice asked.

When I broke from Guy's gaze, I found Devon standing right behind him, Clara only a few steps back.

"What are you doing here?" I asked, instead of answering his question.

"Your mom called and told me about what happened with Nym, and I wanted to help. I figured that's why you came back, but…"

"Yeah, I don't want to talk about that right now."

"I can help with that," Devon said and attempted to nudge Guy out of the way.

"I've got it," Guy protested. "I definitely don't need *your* help."

The numbness in my arm was subsiding, followed by heat and intense tingling as it came back to life. I lightly moved my fingers, and when I wasn't shocked by a lightning bolt of pain, I tried moving my wrist.

"There. Good as new," Guy said.

When he arose, I noticed most of the group had ventured back to the rock mountain and formed a semi-circle around me, curious and concerned as to my condition.

I put pressure on my healed hand, attempting to rise. My butt was badly bruised, and I thought twice about asking Guy to heal me there too just to get another rise out of Devon. However, even I'd seen enough fighting for one night. The bruises were pain I could deal with.

Ivanic was still in his cougar form, apparently not wanting to expose himself to the whole group—or maybe that was upon Razielle's insistence. Though unlike everyone else, his focus was not on me. He was staring down Devon with bared teeth and a low growl.

Razielle tried to calm him, but he wasn't listening.

"Ivanic, that's enough," I said. I thought his over-protectiveness of me would have lessened now he had a girlfriend, but he was seemingly loyal to a fault. This was why I never doubted Clara being able to steal him away from Razielle. However, Devon was another story.

The angry cougar didn't follow my instructions,

either. Devon looked at him, back to me, then began to understand what had Ivanic so pissed.

"I guess my help is no longer required," Devon said, taking the hint.

"It never was," Guy quipped.

Devon opened his mouth, about to respond—eager to argue—but bit his tongue instead. He gave me a final sorrowful glance before returning through the open seam Quin had created. Clara followed him into the void without speaking a word, her expression unreadable.

Ivanic stalked up to the seam, sniffing the air. I couldn't tell if he could actually see the blue gash in midair or he was simply stopping where Devon's scent vanished.

"Who was that guy?" Mom asked. "He looked vaguely familiar, but I can't place him."

I shrugged. "He didn't look familiar to me, but I was his apparent target. No idea why."

"You *have* pissed off a lot of people in your life," Razielle said. "I suspect you can't remember them all."

"Very true. Thanks for that."

"Okay," Mom said. "You all should remain inside the academy walls where it's safe. That guideline always applies, but it's even more important now with this mysterious man on the loose. I'll talk to Headmistress Christi. I know the protection spell has been heightened, but perhaps more can be done to ensure he can't get on campus. Maybe she can get approval to extend the spell to the village."

Everyone talked over each other with questions and concerns, all wanting their voices heard. However, it soon became ambient noise.

I found Nym in the crowd, backing away to get the space she'd originally wanted. There was certainly no leaving her out here now, which I'd told her even before we were attacked.

"Then let's go," I said. "I should close up this seam before the headmistress arrives and starts questioning us."

I helped with guiding my friends who were unable to see the glistening seam transition into the village, the protection spell preventing seams inside the academy walls.

I thanked Mom, Guy, and Quin for their help once we were on the other side of the seam, at the tree line behind a row of townhomes.

Just as I'd been practicing, I released my needle and sewed up the shimmering blue seam, a practice even easier in the darkness since it was clearly visible when my stitchwork wasn't tight enough.

"It's never a dull moment with you around," Guy said to me as our group trekked through the snow to reach one of the main streets.

"I wouldn't mind a little boredom once in a while," I replied with a chuckle.

"How's the hand?"

I stretched my fingers again and rotated my wrist. "Like you said, good as new."

Guy smiled. "Good. Just checking."

We all stopped in the street before parting ways. Mom stepped forward to give me a tight hug, which I eagerly returned.

"Please stay inside the academy walls," she said, talking into my ear. "When you want to visit the village, then please let me or your father know and don't come alone."

"Sure, Mom. I'll be sure to use the buddy system going forward," I said, rolling my eyes, which she luckily couldn't see with her head still resting on my shoulder.

However, she was able to sense my sarcasm. When she finally released me from the embrace, she firmly gripped both of my arms. "I'm not going to treat you like a child, but want you to be safe."

"I know, and I will be." I gave her a solemn nod, attempting to show I was serious. No more sarcasm, which was a persistent struggle for me.

Convinced with my sincerity, Mom allowed my roommates and me to make our way back to the academy—our gang of sapient thugs. I could tell she wanted to walk us back to the gate but trusted us enough to make the short walk together.

When we got back to our room, Nym stopped before the door, silently scrutinizing the cleaning job Mom had done as if she could still make out the words. If she could, then her vision was a hell of a lot better than mine because the door looked perfect to me.

Then, Razielle barreled past and entered. "You girls coming or not?" she asked, holding the door open.

"Recall the amazing things you did tonight and tell me you still consider yourself a monster," I said.

"Being burned really hurts," Nym said.

"Tell me about it." I'd been set on fire nearly every day for weeks in the simulation. The real Tarquin had set me on fire in Ogginosh. My hands had been burned in the first Battle of Spellcrest. So, I could sympathize. Simulation or real, protection spell or no, getting burned always hurt like hell.

CHAPTER 22

*N*ym coming to the cafeteria for any meal was becoming less prevalent. She still had to eat, though I didn't know for how much longer. The transition progressed at different rates for different people, so there wasn't an exact timeline for when it would be complete. Her transformation to vampire would culminate when her mortal heart stopped beating, giving her the pivotal moment when her mortal body died, then her vampire heart would start and Nym would be reborn.

When this defining moment would happen was nothing more than an educated guess. And since she was one of the *lucky* students turned by the plague vampires—potentially even the chairman himself—Nym's moment of rebirth would be even more speculative.

Nym's more frequent absences were always felt, but it was all the more noticeable today at lunch. Razielle shared Non-Magical Studies with her in fourth period, and no amount of insisting brought Nym to the cafeteria.

"How's Nym doing after what happened yesterday?" Sarah asked. Sarah and Bree were the only ones in the group who didn't share a class with Nym this year.

"Nym was never an open book," Razielle said. "But it's harder to tell now more than ever. Don't you agree, Maeve?"

I'd barely seen her since the three of us left for first period. The only class I shared with Nym was Combative Casting, which made lunches way too damn short. But our little elf seemed no worse for wear upon waking up this morning. Even though she'd turned down a proper breakfast, she'd picked up a coffee on the way to her first class, Multi-World History.

"She's strong," I said. "She's proven it many times, but last night especially. I'm confident she'll be fine. You're right—it's often hard to tell what's going on inside that elven head of hers, but she'll make it through her transition as well as anyone."

"I just hope her family finally comes around," Razielle said. "I know it weighs on her."

"She does have support from her family. It's us. We're her family now."

"Anything on who wrote on your door last night?" Ivanic asked.

Razielle and I both shook our heads. Mom was looking into it, of course. She said she'd talk to the headmistress and get with security, which probably also meant getting Devon involved.

He'd texted me this morning, but I'd ignored him thus far, not ready for him to explain himself yet. I was still too upset with what I'd seen to be able to listen. Clara had been in Divination, but hadn't made eye contact with me the whole period.

"I think we should request a hallway camera," Razielle said, then took a long sip from her soda. She didn't have much food on her tray, but hadn't started with much, either. Those of us with fifth-period Combative Casting had transitioned from equal lunch and dinner portions to small lunches and large dinners. I'd also fallen into that category.

"A hidden one," I added. "No use announcing it if we want to catch the culprit."

"We don't need approval from the headmistress for that. Can't your boyfriend do it? He bugged your room, remember?"

"Devon did what?" Sarah asked.

"It was nothing," I said, not wanting to get into that chapter of our murky history.

"He was spying on Maeve during the time she had her own room when we were neophytes," Razielle said. "I don't remember why exactly. It was at the headmistress's request, wasn't it? Not that it made it any better."

I sighed, feeling put on the spot. "It was when I'd lost my needle. My brother had been returned to me, then I'd been hiding my mother when she came back. The headmistress thought I was hiding things from her."

"You were," Razielle said.

"I know, and so was Devon. So, even though he'd installed cameras in my room, he was only giving the headmistress abridged information."

"Still sounds shady to me," Erik chimed in.

"He's always been shady," Ivanic said, followed by a low growl in the back of his throat as he fought to keep the cougar calm. "I never trusted him."

"He's had a complicated life and has been forced to make tough choices," I said, sounding as though I was defending the actions that had broken us up the first time way too much.

I should just stop talking.

"I don't remember hearing about any of this," Bree said. "So, what happened."

With another sigh, I continued. "I found out, we fought about it, and he removed them. That was also when I was given approval to move back in with Razielle and Nym."

"That's right," Razielle said with a growing smile. "And we've been inseparable ever since."

"I wish we could have remained roommates,"

Bree said, glancing at Sarah. "I guess it still pays to have connections."

"Don't look at me," Razielle scoffed. "My connections don't get me squat here."

"But didn't your dad get you back in Spellcrest after being expelled?" I asked.

"Oh yeah... I *did* get expelled." Razielle looked thoughtfully into the distance. "I guess I was starting to remember it as happening to someone else. Damn, were my parents pissed."

With the conversation moving to Razielle, the subject of Devon installing hidden cameras in my room was quickly forgotten, and I was relieved to move on.

With the thought of Nym and the graffiti incident still weighing heavily on my mind, I told everyone I had something to take care of before Combative Casting and left the cafeteria early. A part of me wanted to check in on Nym, but another part thought I could do more good heading in the opposite direction. So, I marched straight for the Manor, aware of the limited time I had.

I peered into Memorial Hall after watching a pair of students turn in and begin browsing the animated murals. A few others milled about farther down the hall, a trio even giggling as they gazed upon the pictures of at least one fallen student.

Their lack of respect made me think they were

neophytes, but I could've been wrong. So much about Memorial Hall enraged me.

As much as I wanted to crack some underclassmen skulls together, I needed to stay on task. I hadn't come to the Manor to pay my respects to Memorial Hall but to confront the headmistress about how Nym was being persecuted at this academy.

Once I reached an area of the hallway where I found myself alone, I teleported to the fifth floor, directly outside the headmistress's invisible office door. I didn't have an appointment, but was sure she was there—I could feel her needle nearby, a skill I'd been getting more practice with.

I pulled the door into existence and ascended the spiral staircase, emerging through the floor of her tower office. She didn't seem to care for the walls being transparent lately, instead going for the castle motif with the circular walls of gray brick. The golden chandelier overhead shone brightly to make up for less natural light flooding the space.

"Like mother, like daughter," she said, looking up from the long conference table. A bowl of soup was set before her, and she sipped daintily from her ornate spoon. "Always arriving unannounced."

"If I announced myself, you'd probably decline the meeting," I said, approaching the table.

"After all this time, you think I'd simply decline a

meeting request from you? I'm here to help and to serve. And you're not just *any* student. You're a seamstress-in-training."

With a wave of her hand, a chair adjacent to where she was sitting pulled back from the table. "Have a seat. I don't know if you've eaten, but if you're hungry, I have extra soup on the desk."

"I'm good," I said, but took the chair I was offered. "So, if my mother was already here, what did she have to say?"

"She informed me that you and some of your friends were outside the academy wall. After all we've been through, I shouldn't have to tell you how unwise that is."

"But did she tell you why we were outside the wall?" I leaned my elbows on the table.

"She told me about a harassment incident, which I am personally looking into, as well as an attack, which security is currently looking into. Whomever it was should not be able to get on campus, so as long as you remain within the academy walls, you have nothing to fear." Headmistress Christi took several more sips from her bowl.

"When are you going to get Nym's name removed from Memorial Hall?" This was the question that brought me here, and I didn't have time to beat around the bush.

"We've already discussed this," the headmistress said in a frustrated tone. "It's a delicate matter and I need majority approval. As I told you before, it will take time, but rest assured, I'm working on it. I'm championing for your friend."

I now wished I'd taken a picture of the writing on our dorm room door. "Nym doesn't feel safe in her own dormitory. After last night's stunt, she's afraid the whole student body is against her. With her tribute in Memorial Hall, she thinks the whole staff is against her. Her parents don't want her home. She's got nowhere to go. You've got to do—"

"This academy has a zero-tolerance harassment and discrimination policy. Whoever is responsible for the intolerable actions from last night will be punished."

"Will they be expelled?"

Headmistress Christi didn't immediately answer, which told me the answer was *no*. "It will depend on who the perpetrator or perpetrators are. I cannot promise you that will be the outcome, though it *is* a possible outcome."

"When I find out who they are, I'll make them wish they were expelled," I warned. "That's something I can promise."

"You will do no such thing, unless you want to find yourself under the same disciplinary action review. Retaliation is an equally punishable offense."

"Then keep them away from me if they continue to attend this academy."

"I know you're just looking out for your friend,

and as admirable as that is, know when to step aside and let the professionals handle the situation." She took a final sip of soup, then placed the spoon in the empty bowl. "This is also an important lesson for a seamstress. You can't do everything yourself. Sometimes, you will require help. Sometimes, you will be required to step aside and let others take over. From your upbringing, I know this is a difficult concept for you."

"What the hell do you know about my upbringing?" I spat. "You were the one who kept me from attending this academy. I should have been enrolled four years earlier. My tuition was paid for. I wasn't recruited because of *you*. If it hadn't been for Helena passing her needle on to me, who knows if I ever would have heard about this place?"

Headmistress Christi seemed taken aback by my outburst. She remained quiet for a long time, sitting perfectly upright in her chair, thoughtfully considering a response.

"There's so much I wish I could explain," she finally said. "I understand your frustration—for your advocating for your friend, your delayed enrollment to this magical institution, and so much more." Her attention turned to the nearby hutch, housing many of the chess piece totems she'd collected throughout the years. "A lot goes into heading this academy and the seamstress council. Much privileged information I am not at liberty to divulge at this time.

"But remember, you are also a seamstress. In time, you will gain access to some of this privileged information. You'll just have to be patient—patience you'll also need as I work to right the wrongs done to your friend Nym." Another pause. "Do you trust me? Do you trust I'm working for you?"

Usually, when someone asked me to trust them, it was a clear sign that I shouldn't. And the head-mistress had given me many reasons not to trust her over the past few years. However, now there was a sincerity in her voice I couldn't deny. I didn't know what to make of her anymore.

"Yes," I said, against my better judgment.

"Good. Then trust I'm working as quickly as I can. I want these things resolved as much as you do."

I doubted that, but didn't make the argument.

"Isn't your next class starting soon?" the head-mistress asked, glancing at a clock on the wall.

With under five minutes to reach Combative Casting, it was time to thank the headmistress for her time and get moving.

With so many students in the halls now, tele-porting wouldn't be the best choice, so I hoofed it down the stairs, headed for the main entrance of the Manor. I couldn't help but glance down Memorial Hall as I passed, hoping it would be fixed soon. Then I could feel as if I'd succeeded in something.

However, gazing down the second hallway, I saw

something I wasn't prepared for, and my heart leapt into my throat.

Nym stood before her remembrance, punching and slashing with incredible force and determination—doing everything she could to erase herself from the memorial.

CHAPTER 23

*S*everal students were positioned farther down the hallway from Nym, watching as my friend violently defaced school property. Not only were they watching, but they were recording the entire scene on their phones.

No one dared approach her, which I was thankful for because she was bound to attack another person as viciously as the wall in which she was currently directing her rage.

But it was only a matter of time before a professor—or the headmistress herself—found Nym in this hysterical state and put an end to it... or an end to her...

I had to take my chances with the little elf. Hopefully, she wasn't too far gone to recognize me as a friend.

"Nym, stop!" I yelled and rushed to her.

Nym didn't acknowledge my presence. In fact, her assault on the wall only seemed to intensify.

I stopped a few feet away, out of striking range and tried again. "Nym, you have to stop this! Look at me!"

When she still didn't listen, I took drastic action by summoning an energy ball and firing it at her. Due to the adrenaline rush fueling her system, she was barely fazed, but finally realized I was here.

Her wild eyes found mine, but there was no recognition in them, just feral rage. She growled at me with a guttural sound that rivaled Ivanic's cougar, a clear warning to stay away. Then she returned her onslaught against the wall, tearing away embedded pictures of the three of us with nails that had turned into claws.

She's not gonna make this easy.

All thoughts of getting to class were gone, replaced by the singular focus to bring my friend back from the brink of insanity. She was being eaten up inside, but I'd never imagined this...

More students were gathering as the time approached for fifth period to start. All the commotion was bound to alert the staff, if they hadn't been already.

I lunged for my friend from behind, tightly wrapped my arms around her body and desperate arms, locked my hands together, and held on for dear life.

Nym roared and thrashed to throw me off, and in doing so, entangled our legs, and sent us both sprawling to the ground. My grip held, so I forced her to fall onto me. Our skulls collided with one another before mine also hit the tile floor.

"Stop fighting!" I breathed, the wind partially knocked out of me.

But I continued to hold her tight.

Like a trapped animal, she bucked and kicked, trying to break my hold as if her life depended on it.

"Let go of me!" Nym growled in a voice I hardly recognized.

"I'm not trying to hurt you!" I said, though she wasn't the one who sounded injured. "Stop fighting me!"

She rolled one way, then the other, trying to find a better point of leverage to break my hold. I was afraid she might turn to more magical means to break free—like setting me on fire—but on some level she seemed to realize I wasn't her enemy.

Just when my strength was ready to give out, with my sweaty hands starting to slip, Nym's fighting to free herself lessened. With the decreased strain on my arms, I was able to keep my hands locked together and remain in control. This time also gave me a chance to recover from the fall, any dizziness from slamming my head multiple times also diminishing.

Finally, Nym's body began to shudder as she was

overtaken by uncontrollable sobbing. I let her go, and she rolled to one side and covered her face with both arms. Even after everything we'd been through, this was yet another side of her I'd never seen. I pushed up to a seated position and gazed down on her with so much empathy that tears started to form in my own eyes.

I wanted to yell at all the onlookers to get the hell out of here, but it wouldn't do anything. They'd continue to stare and record, and I'd become the next crazy meme. We were in a public place, so we couldn't demand privacy. Though maybe Nym's breakdown would show her human side and convince more people to rally behind her than condemn her as the next academy threat.

I gently placed a hand on her side. "It's okay," I said, softly. "Everything's going to be okay."

Nym shook her head but couldn't get any words out amidst her crying.

"Why aren't all of you in class?" a demanding voice said, from the adjacent hallway. A moment later, the headmistress stepped into view, causing the remaining spectators to scatter. "Show's over. Get to class."

Headmistress Christi sauntered into Memorial Hall and took in the scene—from the destroyed wall to the destroyed student sobbing on the floor, with me amidst the destruction.

"I told you this was a problem," I said, trying not

to sound overly critical and justified in my statement.

"I'm aware," she said, examining the wall more closely, then coming to kneel beside Nym. The headmistress gripped one of Nym's arms and pulled it away from her face. "Look at me, sweetie." She waited for Nym to obey. Then the next words out of her mouth greatly surprised me. "This isn't your fault. Do you understand me? It isn't your fault, but you still must deal with it. Things will get harder before they get better. I know that's something you don't want to hear, but it's true. And with that, you must also believe things will get better. Your transition does not mark the end but the beginning."

The headmistress pulled Nym to a seated position, who was now aggressively wiping away her tears. I wrapped both arms around my friend and hugged her tightly, eager to give her the support she so desperately needed.

"What do you have this period?" the headmistress asked.

"We both have Combative Casting," I said since Nym was still having trouble speaking.

"Good. Maeve, why don't you go to class and tell Professor Ocumulus that Nym is meeting with me. She is excused for the day." Headmistress Christi stood, then pulled Nym to her feet, forcing me to let her go.

"Nym, are you okay?" I asked, trying to get her to look me in the eyes.

"She'll be fine," the headmistress answered. "We'll have a short chat, then I'll release her to go back to her room and rest. Go, Maeve. Thank you for your help, but I'll take it from here."

Even though she still didn't say a word, Nym briefly looked my way and nodded. As much as I didn't want to leave her, I felt she couldn't be in safer company than with the headmistress. I didn't believe Nym would get reprimanded for her outburst, and perhaps the headmistress could make some progress reversing my friend's sinking self-confidence.

"I'll be back to the room right after class," I promised and took my leave at the headmistress's insistence.

Most of the student body was back in class, leaving much of the campus empty, which made it safer to teleport. I had a bit of a headache from the fall earlier, so it took nearly three times as long as usual to harness the concentration to transport myself from the steps of the Manor to the basement of Shadow Peaks Hall. However, I still saved a good five minutes of walking. Teleporting was amazing for time management, but terrible for cardio.

I entered the classroom as the last of the students stepped into their simulation pods. I couldn't exactly blend in venturing into the classroom alone, but didn't need to hide. I had a valid excuse for my tardiness.

"Do you have a note, Miss Rainley?" Professor Ocumulus asked, standing by the elaborate station of computers and simulation engineers.

"A verbal one," I said. "From Headmistress Christi. She's also meeting with Nym, so she won't be coming to class today. I got here as fast as I could."

"Well, the simulations just began, so you can still jump in. Get some practice in. Your pod should be ready to go." Professor Ocumulus pointed to my pod, then turned back to the computer screens, looking over one of the—Elliott's shoulder.

Instead of heading to my designated pod, I wandered over to the computer station. "What do you guys do while we're in there?"

The professor looked startled to find me standing a few steps from him, which appeared rather comical given his monstrous stature. "Oh..." he said, sounding flabbergasted. "It's all very technical, but we're monitoring your vitals and reactions to the surrounding inputs. We adjust as needed to keep the experience in line with the baseline metrics, and amp it up as necessary to keep you progressing."

"So, you're continually making it harder on us."

"As you get better, the simulation gets harder," the professor explained. "The experience shouldn't feel progressively harder because your skills are improving. However, there are those students who do not initially progress, have extreme difficulties with the program, and we must dial back the intensity. Each student is different, so we must treat each student and simulation individually."

Angry beeps sounded from one of the computers. Professor Ocumulus moved closer to the alert and inquired about the issue with that station's SE.

"What's happening?" I asked.

"A student's heartrate is too high," Elliott said, who was now closest to me. "We'll pump in a calming agent into the pod to bring it back into the safe range."

"Who is it?"

"I don't know." Elliott looked toward the other computer, but the professor's immense body was blocking his view. "I can't see the screen."

"You don't have all the information on your own computer?" I asked, peering in closer to see what I could determine.

"I don't have them all pulled up. We each focus on a few students at a time. We split up the work to make it manageable." Elliott glanced back at me, his gaze connecting with mine until he happened to glance south. I'd been leaning forward to better see his screen, but his glance prompted me to return to my full height. Elliott noticed my reaction, and he quickly returned his attention to his screen.

I scanned the computer station area more while

the professor and SEs were preoccupied with the running simulations. I'd never really gotten a chance to explore this area of the classroom because I'd always been in the pod like every other student in the class.

Then my attention landed on a small, framed picture hanging on the wall over one of the humming mainframe units. The photograph contained four men standing in a row, smiling for the camera. Professor Ocumulus stood out like a sore thumb due to his size, standing second from the left, but he looked much younger and neatly trimmed. I didn't recognize two of the other men in the picture, but the thinner man standing to Professor Ocumulus's right, each with arms around each other, looked strangely familiar.

"Who's in that picture?" I asked Elliott, pointing to the wall.

Elliott looked up from his screen and followed to where I was pointing. "Oh, that's Professor Ocumulus and his brother, Headmaster Gilroy, and Professor Speaks—the original head of Shadow Peaks Hall—from whom it derived its current name. He was an odd character from what I've been told, nicknamed *the shadow*. Hence, Shadow Peaks."

Elliott was interested to talk about Professor Speaks, and he was also the man who had my attention glued to the picture.

"Where is Professor Speaks now?" I asked, still

unable to look away at that younger, happier face smiling at the camera.

"He's dead," Elliott replied, lowering his voice. He glanced over at the professor, who was still focused on one of the other computers even though the angry beeping from earlier had stopped. "He's been dead a long time—several decades, if I remember correctly. Around a similar time to the professor's brother. Like his brother, Professor Speaks isn't talked about much these days."

However, if this mysterious Professor Speaks was dead, then why were my friends and I fighting him outside the wall last night? And why was he seemingly after *me*?

CHAPTER 24

I didn't go into the simulation after my heart nearly stopped from seemingly identifying the man in black from a picture in Professor Ocumulus's classroom. It was possible it wasn't him—he was instead using transfiguration magic to cover his true identity—but I had no idea how to decipher such things. When it came to magic, so much of what was true could be concealed.

I decided I needed to learn more about Professor Speaks—the mysterious shadow professor. It was best to start with Mom because she always knew more than she let on, and what she didn't, she had better access to find out.

I didn't tell Razielle my findings when we left class together. She was thrilled to have succeeded in her simulated mission again, as did Erik. After Razielle confronted me about Nym's and my absence from the start of class, which I didn't go into detail on, she was eager to turn the conversation back to herself and regale us with her triumph in the simulator.

When we got back to our room, Nym was thankfully already there, huddled on her bed, back against the wall.

"I'm getting better at this simulation thing," Razielle exclaimed, trying to get Nym excited for her. She dropped her backpack at the side of her desk and plopped down into her office chair. "You should have been there."

"I'm glad you're having a fun time with it," Nym said.

"I wouldn't call it *fun*, per se, but I am back to kicking some serious ass."

"And kicking ass is fun," I added.

"Maeve said you met with the headmistress. What was that about?" Razielle asked.

Nym glanced at me before speaking, unsure of what I'd told our Nephilim roommate. "About the situation from last night. Maeve's mom told her about it, so she wanted to check in on me." Her gaze returned to me, as if looking for validation of her response.

"How'd it go?" I asked.

"Good. She's really nice," Nym said. "Not what I expected after everything you've said about her over the past few years. She really seems to care."

"Then why did she let Memorial Hall get built the way it did?" Razielle retorted. "If she cared so much, it seemed as though she would have been more involved and nixed some of the names included—like yours."

I didn't have an answer for either one of them.

I didn't know why the headmistress hadn't been more involved with the choices for Memorial Hall, and why she'd practically returned from the dead a different person, but one who knew way too much to actually *be* a different person.

These were things I couldn't explain, so I wasn't even going to try.

"So, your meeting went well?" I asked Nym, hopeful.

She seemed in much better spirits than when I'd found her defacing her name and pictures. She'd been rabid—seeing red instead of me.

"I think so," Nym said, as noncommittal as ever. "How's your head?"

"What happened to your head?" Razielle asked, suspiciously. Her gaze oscillated between us, knowing there was something we weren't telling her.

"Funny story," I said, and with Nym's permission, let our roommate in on the situation that *actually* led to Nym's meeting with the headmistress.

Razielle's excitement from earlier was gone, and she seemed mostly upset that she hadn't been involved in the incident, almost as though I'd ditched her again. It was a totally different situation, but Razielle didn't see it that way.

"Nym, I saw you right before lunch," Razielle said, sounding hurt. "Why didn't you say anything to me? I could have helped. I could have been there for you."

"I'm sorry," was all Nym could manage to say. "It wasn't a plan or anything... it just sorta happened."

"I discovered something interesting in Combative Casting," I said, attempting to get the spotlight off Nym, knowing I could grab Razielle's attention with a shiny new subject. "Do either of you know how Shadow Peaks got its name? I mean, the other two underclassmen dormitories were named after their founders. But Shadow Peaks didn't seem to fit."

Razielle shook her head. "I guess I never really thought about it—or more likely, I never cared enough to think about it."

"They never mentioned it on the campus tour from the beginning of school," Nym said. She was hugging her knees and rocking slightly. "But it sounds like you learned something."

"Indeed, I did," I said with a satisfied grin. "It's apparently named after Professor Speaks, nick-named *The Shadow*. S. Peaks. The Shadow. Shadow Peaks. Who knew, right?"

"Why was he nicknamed *The Shadow?*" Nym asked.

"I don't know," I admitted. "That's all I currently know about him other than he supposedly died a long time ago—oh, and interestingly enough, he fits the description of the man who attacked us last night."

Both roommates' mouths dropped open in similar shock. "What?" Razielle said.

I realized I was pacing before the beds and stopped. "There's a picture of him in the Combative Casting classroom, over by the computers. He looks younger in the picture, but the resemblance is uncanny."

"Maybe it's a relative," Nym offered.

"You could be right, little elf," I said.

"Or it could be someone who transferred their soul into his body—like with you and your mother," Razielle said.

"That's true too. I hadn't considered that."

Now, things were getting complicated. This man could be anybody. With magic involved, nothing was what it appeared to be. I no longer knew what to believe. However, even if the man in black we fought was not the deceased Professor Speaks, I had to think he was still an important piece to the puzzle—not just some innocent bystander.

"My brain hurts," Razielle complained. "Things

seemed so normal until I started going to school here."

"Mine too," Nym said. "I wouldn't be a vampire, for one. I wonder what my life would be like right now if I'd gone to school abroad."

My life hadn't been normal, but sure as hell hadn't been magical.

As challenging and complicated as my life had become, I wouldn't trade it in for my previous life for anything in the world, when it was just Finley and me.

"I know it's hard for you, but I'm glad you're here," I said. "Spellcrest wouldn't be the same without you—either of you."

Razielle eagerly agreed, but Nym was clearly torn. A part of her wanted to agree with my statement, but if there was a way to have prevented or cure her vampire affliction, we all knew she wouldn't hesitate to do it.

Nym was about to say something when there was a loud knock at the door.

We all looked at each other, determining if any of us were specifically anticipating visitors. Ivanic was always a possibility, especially since it was nearing dinnertime. I wondered when Devon would simply show up to provide an explanation or apology for last night's dinner debacle. But when I opened the door, I was thrilled to realize neither of my guesses had been right. The figure standing in the hallway truly was a pleasant surprise.

"Now, there's a face I wasn't expecting to see today," I said with a smile and stepped aside, so Nym could see who'd come to visit her.

"Toby…" she said, her lips also curling into a smile, revealing the tips of her fangs.

"I got here as quickly as I could," Toby said, entering the room hauling a small rolling suitcase. He took a seat next to Nym, causing the mattress to bounce slightly as he adjusted his position.

"I didn't ask you to do that," Nym said.

"You didn't have to. After what you told me about what happened, I had to come. I booked the first flight I could."

"Do you have to fly back right away?"

"I talked to my professors and told them I'd be gone for the rest of the week," Toby said, combing his blond hair out of his eyes. "I'm all yours for the next few days."

"Where are you staying?" I asked.

"I'll find a place in town. I haven't made any arrangements yet."

"Perfect. Then I have some friends who I know will be more than happy to take you in for a few days. Let me make a call."

"You don't have to do that," Toby said, waving me off.

"It's nothing," I insisted, pulled out my phone,

and retreated to the hallway to give Quin a call. As expected, she and Guy were cool with putting up Toby for the remainder of the week. Their town-home had an extra bedroom, so it wasn't as though Toby had to crash on a couch. When I reentered the room, I gave Toby the good news, along with the address and Quin's number.

Then I gestured to Razielle for us to leave the room—to give Nym and Toby some privacy. They hadn't seen each other since the start of the trimester, each of them—or all of us—preoccupied with the increasing difficulties of the school year.

Razielle at first didn't get the subtlety, so I had to beat her over the head with the suggestion. "Hey, let's give these lovebirds some space."

"Oh… yeah, sure," she said. "I was going to check on Ivanic anyway to see if he's ready for dinner. You guys can join us… but you're probably not hungry."

Nym shook her head. "You girls go on ahead."

I literally pushed Razielle out of the room, even with her protesting that she needed her coat. I grabbed it and tossed it to her.

I hadn't seen Nym look this happy in a long time —a big contrast to the frenzy she'd been in this afternoon. I wished the couple a good evening and joined Razielle in the hallway.

"You coming to dinner?" she asked.

I shook my head. "I'm going to meet my parents

for dinner." I needed to talk to Mom about Professor Speaks.

"It's not Sunday," Razielle said with a pout.

"I know," I said. "But I need to talk to them."

"Man, everyone's leaving," Razielle sighed. "Pretty soon, it's just gonna be Ivanic and me."

"Don't be so dramatic. I'm not leaving." I batted her in the arm as we reached the stairs.

"That's how it starts. It used to always only be on Sundays. Now, it's a day other than Sunday. Then it will be increasing nights a week. And before I know it, you'll be there every night. Nym won't be eating anymore. The others in the group will have their excuses. And bam! Just Ivanic and me."

"That's quite the story," I said, taking the stairs more quickly than the moping Nephilim. "Greatly exaggerated though."

"We'll see," she argued, and falling farther behind —creating more distance between us as if to better prove her point.

I stopped and turned on the stair I was currently on. "Do you want me to come to dinner? I can visit my parents afterward."

"Whatever. You already made the plans. I don't want you to change them for me."

Actually, I hadn't. My parents had no idea I was planning to come over, but it wasn't like they'd turn me away for showing up on their doorstep unannounced.

"I'll join you for dinner," I said. "Okay? Happy now?"

"If you really want to." Razielle shrugged.

I groaned. "After all these years, why do I still let you get your way? You're like a toddler."

"But you love me," Razielle grinned.

I laughed at her innocent smile, the two of us heading to Ivanic's room. I'd call Mom after dinner to tell her I was coming over. She'd want to meet me in the square, so I wouldn't be walking so far alone, then I'd have to remind her that I could easily teleport.

She didn't need to worry. I was on guard—ready for anything. I had no intention of venturing too far from campus. The man in black—whoever he was—wouldn't sneak up on me again. I knew his face now, whether it was really his or not. I could see him coming.

CHAPTER 25

"What are you doing here? It's not Sunday," I said to Finley when he answered the door of my parents' townhome.

"I could ask you the same thing," he said. He didn't immediately step aside to let me in, so I pushed right past. "I like to visit sometimes without everyone else."

Mom came down the stairs to meet me in the living room. The television was on, playing some dramatic superhero show. The few seconds I saw didn't tell me anything. I couldn't keep up with all the shows being released these days.

"Did you want some dessert?" Mom asked after giving me a hug.

"I'm not one to turn down dessert," I said.

"Mom, do you want me to pause it?" Finley asked.

"No, you go ahead and keep watching." She led the way into the kitchen and headed to the refrigerator. "I'm not used to you coming over outside of Sundays."

"What about Finley?"

"He usually stops by once or twice a week... especially on weeks your father's gone."

"Dad's not here? Where is he?" I asked.

Mom pulled a pumpkin pie out of the fridge. "Ice cream too?"

"Why is that even a question?"

"I guess I forgot who I was talking to," Mom laughed and dug into the freezer for a carton of ice cream. "Your father's in Kicryria with Guy. He'll be back this weekend."

"I see." So, Guy was gone too. I hoped Nym wouldn't mind that her boyfriend would be sharing a townhouse with only Quin. If I had known, I probably wouldn't have offered. However, I didn't want to retract the offer now, confident they were both trustworthy adults.

Mom cut me a slice of pie and set a scoop of chocolate chip ice cream on the side, then handed me the plate. Afterward, she cut a sliver for herself. "I already had dessert," she said, justifying her minuscule serving size. "But I couldn't let you eat alone."

"Mom, you're missing everything," Finley called

from the living room. "You're not going to know what's going on."

"I'll catch up later!" Mom yelled back, then sat across from me at the kitchen table. "Has he always been this demanding?"

"No," I laughed. "He's definitely getting worse as he gets older."

Mom chuckled at my comment and took a half-sized bite of her pie. I dug into mine as well, making sure to get equal portions of pie and ice cream on my fork.

Mom was finished with her dessert thirty seconds later, so she started our discussion. "I know you want answers with what happened last night, but I don't have any information to tell you yet. There have not been any suspects identified for vandalizing your door and I don't have any clear information regarding the guy attacking you by the tower ruins. I met with Devon and campus security, who informed me about a werewolf who'd also attacked you and Devon recently. It's more than likely the incidents are related, but it's not confirmed."

"You didn't recognize the man last night?" I asked between bites. "Because it looked to me like you did."

"I'll admit he looked familiar, but I didn't recognize him."

"Well, that's why I'm here—not that I was expecting you to have answers, but to give you information I've learned. What do you know about Professor Speaks?"

"Only that he was the founder of Shadow Peaks Hall," Mom said. "He was before my time by a few years. He died under mysterious circumstances, if I remember correctly."

"You never saw a picture of him?"

"Maybe I did when I was in school—nearly thirty years ago. I can't remember everything I saw or learned back then." Mom stood and dropped her empty plate in the sink. "How's the pie?"

"Delicious," I said. "So, you don't know anything else about him?"

Mom shrugged as she returned to the table.

She pulled her hair out of the toppling bun it was in and fixed it.

"Despite what you may think, I don't know everything about this school. There are plenty of professors—including founding professors—about whom I know nothing, or have never even heard of. After my high-school tenure here, I came back occasionally, but not in any official capacity. Then you know what happened—your father and I were crystallized for over a decade. The time since I've been back has given me a new vantage point of the academy.

"Headmistress Christi has given me a lot of access, but there's a lot about the Academy's history I don't know much about.

"So, no. I don't really know anything about Professor Speaks, but I can research him. What does he have to do with the man who attacked you last night?"

At this point, I thought it would have been obvious—but then again, maybe she just wanted to hear me say it. "He was the one who attacked us, or at least someone who looks like him."

Mom didn't respond.

"I saw a picture in Combative Casting. It looked just like him even though the picture was taken— well, like you said—before your time."

"That's really strange," Mom finally said. "Why would someone be imitating him after all these years? And what's he doing attacking students?"

"Specifically, me," I said. I made my last bite a big one, then set my plate in the sink on top of the one Mom had left in there. "Do I have a stamp on my forehead that says *come and get me* or something? I mean, seriously. This crap is getting old."

"At least this gives me something to go on. I'll ask around and see what I can find out about the old founding professor of Shadow Peaks and see if we can make a connection with the man who attacked you."

Instead of returning to the table, I leaned against the counter and crossed my arms. "Could it really be him?"

"Anything's possible," Mom said. "Give me a few

more days, and when your father gets home, I'll enlist his help too. In the meantime, remain within the Academy walls. I don't want to worry about you. No exploring. You got me?"

I nodded. "I can teleport from here to there no problem. Otherwise, I'll remain on campus."

"Good." Mom rose from the table. "Since you're here, you want to stick around for a while? We can start the show over—or put on a movie."

"Finley will be mad."

Mom shrugged. "One of you always will be."

I laughed at her comment and felt good about irritating the little man.

It was my big sisterly duty I'd been neglecting for quite some time. And besides, I didn't want to interrupt Nym and Toby so soon. "Sure. I'm in."

As expected, Finley complained when I told him we were changing the show, and again when I forced him to move over and stop hogging the whole couch. However, once we were all settled in, there was nothing left to complain about. There was a wonderfully warm feeling at spending an evening with family—not out of obligation, but desire. This was what we had missed growing up, but better late than never.

With the shit I'd dealt with last night, it would be a well-deserved break and relief to watch the drama rather than live it.

CHAPTER 26

*D*espite the events of the past few days, Nym was in a happier mood than I'd seen her since the beginning of the trimester. The tables had turned once again, returning to our original dynamic with Razielle as the queen morning grouch.

"I barely got to sleep," Razielle whined. "It can't be morning already. It's not fair."

"I barely sleep at all anymore, and I'm up," Nym retorted, getting sassier as the vampire in her took hold.

"You're a vampire. You don't have to sleep."

"Close, but not yet."

"From what I could hear, you were sleeping just fine," I said, retrieving my soul crystal from the dresser. I placed it around my neck, tucked the warm crystal under my top, then grabbed my leather jacket. "You're the one keeping the rest of us up."

"That's not true," Razielle argued. "I tossed and turned all night."

"So, you actually snore when you're awake? If it's true, then it's just spiteful." I checked my face in the mirror, shut the cabinet door, and smirked at the Nephilim who'd yet to drag her sorry ass out of bed.

Arguments would finally dry up for most people, but not her. "I don't snore."

"Yeah, you do," Nym said, slinging one strap of her backpack over her shoulder. She wore her winter coat with the furry trimmed hood covering her head. I didn't know if she truly needed it for warmth anymore or if wearing it was simply habit.

Razielle and I shared Divination first period, but I said I wouldn't wait for her to get ready. She could catch up. Maybe that would convince her to complain less in the morning—though I doubted it.

So, while Razielle was deciding what to wear, Nym and I left. We headed to the cafeteria where I'd get breakfast and a sweetened coffee to-go, and Nym would grab a black coffee. She surprised me by getting a toast as well—though she now preferred it burnt and dry, claiming she could barely taste it anyway.

Toby spent the night at Quin's townhouse, and Nym wasn't jealous or suspicious at the fact that Guy was away with my father. She clearly had nothing to worry about, but her reactions to surprises were becoming overreactions and increasingly erratic.

Fortunately, this morning constituted a tally mark in the positive column.

"You and Toby seem to be doing really well," I said as we left the cafeteria, starting our short trek to the Manor. The sky was clear this morning, the sun barely reaching over the whitecapped trees.

"We are," Nym admitted. "I can't believe he flew all the way out here after we got off the phone."

"He's dedicated to you."

"We all have someone dedicated to us now. We're all so fortunate."

"Yeah…" I said, thinking of where I'd left things with Devon—uncertain, to say the least. He was really poking my trust button again, shooting off all kinds of warning bells.

"You don't agree?" Nym asked, suddenly confused.

"No—I mean yes. I do."

She gave me a curious look but didn't press.

It didn't take us long to reach the steep steps of the Manor, and we parted ways once we got inside, Nym off to Multi-World History.

Before I headed for Divination, I stopped at Memorial Hall, curious to see how the damage Nym had caused yesterday had been handled. I ventured down the hallway, unable to see wall damage. Then I realized I also didn't see any mention of Nym.

I stopped before a blank wall—perfectly preserved and painted. I stood before a large unused section between other student remembrances. From my distance to the end of the hall, I was pretty damn confident I was in the right spot. As I looked farther down the hallway, I noticed more blank sections, making the memorial look unfinished. But it wasn't *unfinished*. It was more finished than when it had been opened to the student body.

I was so excited with my discovery, I sprinted to Multi-World History. The bell sounded as I ran, but it didn't deter me to stay the course. I barged into the classroom, causing half the class to take notice.

"Maeve?" Professor Haricot asked.

"Sorry, Professor, but I need to borrow Nym for a minute."

"We're starting class. Can't it—"

"It's important," I urged. "I'll bring her right back. I swear."

"Oh, alright," she sighed. "Please be quick about it."

I promised I would, as long as Nym would hurry along. She was still in her chair, staring at me with concerned and questioning eyes. Reluctantly, she rose and headed for the door as I continued to hold it open. I gestured for the little elf to pick up the pace, so I could keep my promise. I'd have explaining to do by the time I got to *my* class, but I wasn't concerned about the professor's curiosity.

"What's this all about?" Nym asked once we were marching through the empty hallway.

"I can't explain it. I just have to show you," I said with a knowing smile, leading her straight to Memorial Hall. As I turned down the second side, where I'd found her in a frenzy yesterday, she stopped, not wanting to proceed any farther.

"Maeve, what are you doing?" Nym asked, her voice so full of skepticism it broke my heart.

"You have to see this, little elf. I promise it's a good thing," I assured her to get her moving again.

When she still refused to take any more steps, I returned to the end of the hallway and grabbed her hand. She attempted to pull away, but I held firm. With her increased strength, if she'd really put up a fight, she could have physically overpowered me, but she didn't. I towed her along and stopped before the section of wall where her remembrance had been.

"What do you see?" I asked, letting her hand go and giving her space.

"Nothing," Nym said, sourly.

"Exactly. Look around. Look where we are."

It took her a moment of examining the wall before us and down either side.

"It's gone…" Her words were quiet to start, then she found her voice. "It's gone! I can't believe it's gone!" Her lips curled up into the biggest smile I'd ever seen her wear, even as a tear rolled down one cheek. Faster than a typical attack, she turned and threw herself onto me, not realizing her own strength as she squeezed me tight.

"I can't breathe," I wheezed, also trying to get out a laugh.

"I'm sorry," Nym said, immediately easing up, but not letting me go. "The headmistress said she would, but I didn't really believe her. And even if she did, I didn't think it would be so soon."

"I guess she needed to see the damage it was causing you firsthand to kick her old ass into gear."

Nym laughed, released me, then wiped her cheeks with both hands. "Things are starting to look up."

"It's good to finally hear you laugh."

"It feels good to know I still can." She dabbed under her eyes with her middle finger. "My eyeliner isn't running, is it?"

"No. You still look perfectly regal, little elf," I said with a relieved smile.

"Thank you for this, Maeve." Nym pulled me in for another hug, and now I was the one holding her tight.

My phone buzzed in my pocket, but I ignored it.

It had been so long since I'd felt as though I could genuinely hug her.

Ever since she'd been turned, it had been hard to get close to her. She kept everyone at a distance—emotionally and physically. Each time I attempted physical contact, I felt as though I was taking my life in my hands, trying to pet a tiger.

"I promised Professor Haricot I wouldn't keep you long," I finally said after the extended embrace.

Nym didn't answer, but instead went back to staring at the perfectly empty wall. She was alive again in the eyes of the academy, and she looked it. She looked radiant.

"No longer a reason to try and tear down the school with your bare hands," I said. "Now we can get back to what we came here for—to learn and grow our magical abilities."

"Yeah." She glanced at me when she spoke her one-word response, and just as quickly, her attention returned to the wall. The blank canvas.

I had to pull her away and drag her back to class, but again, she wasn't really putting up a fight. When Nym entered the classroom, I waved to Professor Haricot, proceeding to first period.

I checked my phone on the way, and as expected, Razielle had texted me wanting to know where the hell I was. Well, it proved she'd made it to class. No use replying now. I'd see her soon enough.

CHAPTER 27

*I*n Divination, Professor Lin began lecturing on the fundamentals of Augury, or the discipline of interpreting omens through the observation of bird behavior.

Interpreting these omens was called *taking the auspices*. And she listed out the two primary classes of birds for this discipline: Oscines and Alities.

I got to class just in time to catch the end of the introduction before Professor Lin informed us that we'd be going on a field trip, then led us to the forest edge right outside the academy wall. She must not have gotten the memo that we were on unofficial lockdown. Perhaps, the news of the attack hadn't been shared with all professors—though Clara knew, and she said nothing. She'd no more than glanced in my direction since I'd arrived at class.

I was breaking my promise to Mom by being out

here, but figured there was safety in numbers. So, I wasn't concerned about another attack while I was among an entire class of peers and an academy professor.

I guessed Clara accounted for something too, but I mostly wanted to block her out completely.

Even though plenty of birds flew over the academy and nested in the topiaries, the professor insisted the best experience would be to observe these heavenly creatures in their natural habitat. Legend had it, the site of Noctem City was chosen by its vampire founders from an auspice reading—the place where Spellcrest Academy now stood. The plague vampires were no longer around, so there was no one left alive to confirm this legend was true.

"I can't believe you ditched me *again*," Razielle whispered as Professor Lin spoke about the differences in bird songs, movements, and flight patterns. Sarah stood on the opposite side of me, quietly listening in, but not wanting to get in the middle of a roommate squabble.

"I didn't ditch you," I argued. "I told you. I was helping Nym. I wasn't going to call you out of class after discovering the wall had been fixed."

"You called *her* out of class."

"Because it was about *her*." I wasn't going to keep arguing with her about this. It was greatly chipping away at the euphoria I'd felt earlier.

"Whatever. I'm happy for her. But it sucks I missed it. *You* made me miss it."

"We'll celebrate the win later today—*together*. Okay?" I said, trying my best to cheer her up while also defusing the argument. We had to get back to listening to the professor because I had no idea what she was saying.

"Maeve, since you seem to know all this information already, why don't you be our first volunteer?" Professor Lin said, immediately drawing my attention back to the official class conversation.

Great. Just the thing I was trying to avoid. Why couldn't Razielle have an inside voice?

"Volunteer?" I asked, innocently.

"For getting a reading," Professor Lin said.

"No, thanks. I'm good." After my last reading, I couldn't exactly trust the information given by the professor—not that I trusted Divination readings in general.

"I insist." The professor waved me over, instructing a few students standing in front of me to step aside, so I could approach.

Clara gazed out into the forest, seemingly ignoring me as much as I was her.

As a cluster of students parted, a clear path to the professor emerged.

"Good luck," Razielle said.

"This is your fault," I seethed.

"You'll be fine," Sarah said in her most reassuring voice.

"No. I'd call it karma for ditching me," Razielle said in response to my comment. She folded her arms across her chest and challenged me with a sneer.

It was no use arguing. I'd lost this battle.

I crunched my way through the snow to stand beside Professor Lin.

"What good is me getting a reading if you're not going to tell me the truth about what it is?" I asked, looking the professor dead in the eyes.

"What would cause you to insinuate I wouldn't tell you a truthful reading?" she asked, not shying from my intended gaze. The students gathered around us became deathly quiet.

"In my last reading, you said I would be tested before the new moon. I remembered you looking like you were holding something back." I glanced at Clara before continuing. She wasn't ignoring me now. "Then Miss Long came to me after class and said tested wasn't the right word. The true reading was that I'd be *attacked* before the new moon. And you know what? I was."

Professor Lin was momentarily speechless. She glanced at her uncomfortable TA as she considered her rebuttal. "Was your attack not a test?" she finally asked, justifying her original reading. "Are all attacks not tests of some kind? Remember, all disciplines of Divination carry varying degrees of interpretation. A word can be exchanged—with a similar one, with a similar connotation—altering the context of the reading.

"This doesn't make the reading fabricated or a fallacy. Each of you in this class should understand this by now. And our lovely new TA has no excuse for discrediting one interpretation for another." The professor eyed Clara as she delivered the blow of her final line.

"I'm so sorry, professor," Clara said, her gaze dropping to her snow-covered boots. "I—I thought I was helping."

"Undermining my credibility is quite the opposite of helpful."

I couldn't suppress a smile, nor did I want to. I was getting far too much satisfaction by seeing her squirm. Maybe this would get her reassigned to another class... or another school. A girl could dream.

"I'll be sure never to do it again," Clara said.

Professor Lin deemed continued scolding of her assistant unnecessary—or inappropriate in front of the whole class—and turned her attention back to me. "Take a look around and tell me what you see."

"What am I looking for?" I asked, though from the snickers behind me, it was apparently a stupid question.

"Birds," the professor said emphatically. "What

we've been talking about for the duration of this class period."

Birds. Of course.

I scanned the tree line, gazing up at the high branches, then up into the clear blue sky. Only small patches of clouds were scattered overhead like fluffy, white islands in the ocean. A hawk or eagle sailed and circled above. I could hear the hammering of a woodpecker echoing from somewhere nearby. Other chirping and cheerful conversations sounded from the trees, and it took some searching to locate a small ash-colored bird.

"There." I pointed to the tree where I'd finally found the small bird standing on a bare branch, chattering with friends I couldn't see. Then I raised my index finger to the hawk still soaring above the trees. "And there."

"Very good," Professor Lin said. "The first one you identified is a gray jay. They're very social creatures, and thus usually found in groups. I see three, but there are most likely a few more nearby. The bird of prey circling is a red-tailed hawk, looking for his breakfast. At least one gray jay has noticed the hawk and is communicating to the others to be careful—keep a watchful eye.

"If you look in the snow by the trunk to your left, you'll notice a white bird doing his best to blend in with its winter feathers. It's a white-tailed ptarmigan. During the summer, it will be streaked with brown and gray. One of its ways to preserve energy in the winter is to roost in snowbanks and avoid flying."

The professor returned her attention to the birds she'd identified, observing them with a keen eye. This was usually the time when she'd ask Clara for her opinion, but not this morning—not after the revelation from earlier.

"You're nothing if not consistent," she said, after interpreting the auspice from the seemingly random collection of birds.

"What's that supposed to mean?" I asked.

"Again, you will be tested—this time, before the spring thaw."

"If that's the true reading, how do you know it applies to me?"

"Because you're the one I'm delivering the reading to. This is not a still life, but a fluid picture—ever-changing like the tide. Intention and the intended recipient provide the specific meaning. The reading I'm delivering is yours. I apologize if it is not to your liking."

"What if you let another few students go, then come back to me?" I asked. "Maybe my luck will change?"

The professor shook her head. "Another reading will offer another result, but doesn't invalidate this one. This reading has already been given life. Any future readings will not extinguish the life of this one."

"Perfect."

"Your test will be presented by a choice," Professor Lin continued. "A choice of how to save someone you love."

"Is that everything?" I wanted out of the spotlight and to return to the back of the class. "Any more omen details you want to share?"

Professor Lin gazed out at the birds for another long, agonizing moment, making me wish I hadn't asked the question. A test? A choice? Anything else? I seriously didn't want to know the answers to any of these questions.

Divination is all bullshit, right?

If I truly believed it, then why was I now trembling? I tried to convince myself it had to do with the cold air of the morning, but it was a weak argument.

"Yes, that is the best of what I can reliably extrapolate from the current scene." the professor said, then paused again. "Perhaps we should save additional readings for tomorrow. It's already getting late."

"Wait," I said as the students started to turn toward the wall. "What are you extrapolating from the scene? What are you seeing?"

My question caused everyone to stop.

The professor offered a small smile. "The hawk

circling overhead denotes danger—either in the form of an attack or a test. The gray jays are aware of its presence, to signify a dangerous situation or test. An attack is usually not seen coming. A test typically provides warning, so some amount of preparation can be made. I received the bit about the choice and saving a loved one from the expressive conversations from our gray jay friends."

"What about the white bird on the ground?"

"The white-tailed ptarmigan." The professor looked over to see if the bird was in the same spot as before. "That's where I extrapolated the timeline. She is waiting—waiting for the snow to melt, for warmer temperatures. This omen will take time to come to fruition, hence the spring thaw."

Waiting was the part I most dreaded. This stupid omen would be hanging over my head for months if I was seriously waiting for the spring thaw.

"Do you have anything to add?" Professor Lin asked Clara.

"No, professor," Clara answered in a quiet voice, refusing to take the challenge. "I have nothing to add."

Satisfied, Professor Lin led the class back inside, and soon we were back within the magical wall of the academy, having returned without a serious incident.

"I'm glad I didn't have to go after your reading,"

Razielle said as we marched back to the Manor. "What do you think it'll be this time?"

I shook my head. "I don't even want to think about it right now." However, my mind was already reeling with sinister scenarios.

CHAPTER 28

*S*tupid omens cursing me at each chance they get.

Professor Lin made it sound as if the only thing separating a test from an attack was semantics. So, my upcoming test could still be an attack—an attack could be a test and a test could be an attack. Now, it didn't matter which one sounded better.

They were apparently interchangeable. And they both sucked.

Much to Professor Haricot's chagrin, I didn't participate in Multi-World History. It didn't matter that we were learning more about Kicryria and my father was currently there.

In Non-Magical Studies, I put my head down on my desk, not even bothering to pretend to pay attention. Professor Thumri didn't call me on it. She didn't want to be in class any more than the rest of us.

On my way to Advanced Evocation, I was stopped by a familiar, yet unwelcomed face. Devon stepped out from Memorial Hall, and our eyes connected while I was still twenty feet away.

I considered ducking into the next hallway I passed—but it ended up being the entrance of Memorial Hall, which would only trap me in with no way of escape. I needed to pass Devon to reach my next class. Who needed Advanced Evo anyway?

Devon waded through the crowd of students between classes to reach me. I was trapped regardless.

"You haven't returned any of my texts," he said, sourly.

"That should tell you something," I said. "I wasn't ready to talk to you yet."

"Well, I am. We can't let a simple misunderstanding get between us. After all we've been through, this is nothing."

"What I saw wasn't *nothing*."

"What you saw was bad timing, nothing more. Nothing was, nor was going to happen." Devon reached for my chin, to lift my head and meet his gaze, but I turned my head in defiance. "You have to believe me when I say there is nothing between Clara and me. There is no *we* concerning her. The *we* is only between you and me."

"I want to believe you," I said. "But it's hard… knowing who she is and what you two shared. And now she's back in your life. It's a lot."

"Maybe the group dinner idea was a mistake." Devon ran a hand through his hair. "I just wanted the two of you to get along. I knew you could…"

"You weren't tempted to kiss her?"

"No."

"You wouldn't have kissed her back if she kissed you?"

"No." His answer was emphatic. "I would have stopped it immediately. I don't believe she would have even let things get that far. She might be a little sad and confused, but I'm not. You're the one I want to be with." Devon stepped closer and placed a warm hand on my arm. His touch always felt good, and this was no exception.

However, when he placed his opposite hand on my waist, I stiffened and stepped back. Devon dropped his hands and his head, frustrated with my continuing to pull away.

"How do you know she won't try again?" I asked. "You might not have been tempted this time, but how do you know you won't be next time?"

"I just know. I don't know what else to say." Devon teetered on his heels. "I love you, Maeve."

Now, I was the one who was a little sad and confused. "I want to believe that too," I said and tried to push past him, but he put up a hand to stop me.

"What do you want me to do?" Devon asked. "Say I'll never see her again?"

"Let me go. I have to get to class."

Devon sighed, then stepped aside. "I'll let you go to class, but won't let you go."

I looked up at him with a sad smile, then took a few steps before getting swept away in the current of students rushing to beat the bell. When I finally glanced back before turning down an adjacent hall-way, Devon was gone.

I couldn't get the image of them with joined hands out of my mind. Maybe it was as innocent as he'd claimed, or maybe they simply hadn't had enough time. I'd sensed their lips getting closer, but had to admit, it could have been projection on my part. Given their history, I'd been paranoid from the moment I'd learned who she was, apart from our Divination TA.

"Why do you look all mopey?" Erik asked, emerging from the depleting student crowd and taking stride beside me. "I figured you'd be thrilled with Nym's removal from the wall of shame. She told me all about it last period."

"Yeah, I'm stoked for her," I said, forcing a smile. "Didn't you have class with Sarah this morning?"

"Multi-World History, second period. She told me about Divination, but it didn't sound so bad."

"Then she must not have told it right."

"It sounded worse for Miss Long. I heard you brutally threw her under the bus."

The comment brought a spiteful smile to my face. "I might have. But regardless, I had other shit come up this morning."

"Oh, sorry. Girl stuff?"

"What? No, not that," I scoffed.

"Okay, then nothing a little Advance Evo can't cure, right?" Erik put an arm around my shoulder, only to remove it a few seconds later as we entered the classroom.

"This class *is* the highlight of my day." As far as classes this year went, it was true. I took my seat beside Bree and greeted Ivanic.

"Nym's news this morning was so awesome," Ivanic said once I got situated. "I'd never seen her so excited in Divination."

"Ivanic told me about it," Bree said, beaming in the seat beside me. "Quite the victory."

"It sure is," I said. "Hopefully, it will take the target off her back."

"Fingers crossed," Erik said.

"Or if we can make an example out of the idiots who graffitied your door, then that'll deter retaliation," Ivanic said. "Have you heard anything yet?"

"No," I said. "It's being investigated. That's all I know. But I'd rather find out before the administrators, so I can kick some cowardly ass."

"I'm in," Ivanic said, seconded by Erik.

"I'm not really into the whole ass kicking thing," Bree said, which no one was surprised to hear. "But I fully support your effort."

"I'm not asking anyone to join me, but won't deny backup," I said.

As Professor Quail instructed us to practice our mental phrase extractions, I was back to working with Bree. I had no desire to do anything dubious this class hour.

Either she figured it out on her own merit, or she didn't. I wasn't going to be behind any magical sleight of hand—for good or bad.

My head was slightly clearer after conversing with my friends, but I still hadn't reclaimed my typical degree of focus. Too many competing thoughts ran through my head—from the Divination omen to my uncomfortable discussion with Devon —which kept me from identifying the phrase I was supposedly listening for.

In the end, I failed, which Bree reveled in more than I appreciated. But I let her have the win without justification or argument. I didn't even try to justify my failure when Bree told the whole group about it at lunch.

"Everyone has an off day," Nym said, noticeably more social today. It was also quite the treat to have her join us for lunch again. She'd decided on her own to come back into the circle. It helped that Toby was still in town, also joining us for lunch.

"You've had a lot of them," Razielle quipped.

"Yes. This is my best day in a long while." Nym and Toby had their entwined hands resting on the table between them. They each had to navigate their lunches with their remaining hands—Toby with his nondominant hand. He was still proficient with his left hand due to the ambidextrous tattoo on his wrist —the one Nym had lost, and I'd missed out on.

I needed both hands for my bean and cheese burrito, which was half the size of my head, so me holding hands with a significant other while I tried to eat was completely out of the question. Not to mention, my significant other and I were not currently on handholding terms.

"Me too," Bree said. "Not only did I kick butt in Advanced Evo, but I rocked it in Combative Casting. And this lunch lasagna is *amazing*. This is, like, the best day ever."

I wish I could agree. But again, I attempted to be happy for those in the group who actually were.

As I looked around the table, it finally hit me that Bree was the only one not officially paired up—and at the moment, neither was I. Sarah and Erik were always precarious. Razielle and Ivanic were going strong. And Nym and Toby were super cute together.

Toby was so attentive and supportive of her; I couldn't help but think how it might have been if we'd gotten together. He'd started by pursuing me while we were pledging S&S and Devon had been out of the picture. Then I'd introduced him to Nym. Razielle had somehow been in the middle of the exchange as well, delirious about the whole S&S prospect and her apparently being a legacy, but that didn't pan out. Nym was the perfect fit, which showed now more than ever.

"For the first time this trimester, I know I can handle the simulator," Nym said, ending the moment when everyone was focused on their food.

"I have every confidence in you," Toby said and kissed the back of her hand.

"Of course, you can," Razielle seconded. "Because you're the baddest bitch in that thing… well, besides me, and sometimes Maeve—though not today."

"*Thanks*," I said, sarcastically, then took a whopping final bite of my burrito. The one thing I wasn't going to do today was sacrifice my lunch for the simulator.

"The best way to kick your ass into gear is by making you feel as though you're coming in second… or third."

The Nephilim had a point. I truly excelled when I was angry, not moping around as I'd done for much of the morning. And I was thinking about so many other things, I was barely giving the simulator any consideration. I'd even eaten a full meal for lunch, which I couldn't have fathomed a few weeks ago.

"Quit picking on Maeve," Ivanic said, mistakenly scolding his girlfriend. "She's had a rough day."

"It's okay," I said. "I can handle it. I can dish it, and I can take it."

"I'm just *testing* you," Razielle said, completely ignoring Ivanic's comment.

"You've tested my patience since day one."

"You arrived super early."

"Which still wasn't my fault." I had to laugh at the grudge she'd continued to hold for two and a half years. "You're never gonna let it go."

"I'll still be reminding you of it when we're hundreds of years old," Razielle said, smirking at me.

And the thought of what she said truly warmed my heart. Throughout all the bickering, she expected us to still be friends hundreds of years from now. We'd talked about our potentially long lifespans as roommates before. Nym would become immortal. Nephilim could live many hundreds of years, if not longer. And seamstresses also had extended lifespans, from what I'd learned. So, from Razielle's perspective, we wouldn't be navigating these long lives alone, but together. It sounded like a life worth living.

"If we're still friends in hundreds of years, then you can remind me of it as many times as you want," I said.

"Of course, we would. Why wouldn't we be?"

Razielle asked as if it was the most obvious and inevitable thing in the world.

"What about me?" Nym asked.

"You'll be there too, though you'll probably outlive all of us."

"How about the rest of us?" Ivanic asked.

"We're all gonna own this school one day," Razielle said. "Run it better than it's ever been run before. It's gonna be amazing. I can see it now. And even though we'll be executives, we'll come back and eat at this very table. It's ours, now and forever."

"Look at you, giving the motivational speech," I said, leaning over to rest my head on her shoulder. "Together forever."

However nice a picture it painted, I didn't know if we'd all stick together long term, but had no doubt about the three amigas. I didn't expect us to be roommates for life, but we'd certainly always be there for each other.

A part of me wanted to skip ahead and find out— whip out my needle and jump to the end of our story —but I didn't want to ruin the surprises along the way. I also didn't want to shake the confidence I now felt with a revelation I couldn't take back.

CHAPTER 29

I didn't start really thinking about the simulator until we reached the basement classroom, and even I was becoming more hopeful. To hell with the frustrations and failures from earlier in the day. I had a full stomach, and this class signified a new start.

Professor Ocumulus greeted us with his warm, booming voice. The moods of many of the students had greatly improved over the weeks, with the members of our group being among them. Even Nym had a subdued sense of excitement.

I placed my valuables in the mailbox and waited for the professor to give the signal. Glancing around the room, my gaze met Elliott's, who'd swiveled around at his station. He gave me a beaming smile and a thumbs up, which I politely returned and turned away. I didn't want to give him the wrong impression. God knew, he was now eager to get my attention.

Professor Ocumulus instructed us to enter our respective pods, and most of the class did so without delay.

"See you on the other side," I said to my friends as I stepped into my white simulator egg. The door closed while I settled in the center of the pod. I closed my eyes and waited for the seamless transition into an elaborate new world. Within seconds, I was once again standing in my safehouse mountain cabin.

I didn't know what awaited me this time on the other side of the door, but I marched straight up to it, leaving all my hang-ups, frustrations, and security behind.

As I stepped through the doorway, the familiar small-town street materialized. I hurried to reach the shop where my parents were shopping, so I'd be standing before them when they exited. When they did, carefree and holding hands, I remained directly in their path to force them to acknowledge me. But still, they didn't—

"Hello, Maeve," Mom said as they both stopped before me. "What are you doing here? You should be in school."

What the hell? This is new.

"We better get you back, on the double, sweetie," Dad said and urged me along.

They walked briskly down the sidewalk and turned into the first alley.

"We can't go that way," I demanded, stopping at the edge of the sidewalk.

"This is the fastest way to our car," Mom said. "We need to get you back to school."

"We can go around—to the next street," I insisted.

"Nonsense," Dad said, starting to sound irritated. "There's no reason to go the long way. Our car's right over here." He led Mom into the alley, and they continued without me.

I knew what was coming next, but didn't cry for them anymore. I'd found a way to disassociate from the simulated versions of them. They were not my parents. And they were programmed to walk this way; there would be no deviation from their preprogrammed path. I knew this. But it still punched me in the gut to see them gunned down seconds later.

Only then did I enter the alley. I was no longer a seven-year-old child rooted to the spot, but a warrior ready to take on anything that engaged. Time wasn't wasted on the original image of the ragged gunman anymore. This man never existed in real life, and no longer existed in the simulation. It was only Tarquin. It had always been Tarquin.

He didn't need a gun, but that was what he used in this fabricated scenario to incapacitate my parents. Still, a bottomless reservoir of blood poured from their bodies and spread like an ocean, overtaking the alley. Tarquin knelt in the rising pool, placing crystals in their mouths to extract their souls before they died.

I shot a fireball to get his attention. He gazed up with wild eyes and a wilder beard that housed small spiders dangling from red thread.

"Have you ever seen arms ripped from a body?" he asked, though his sewn lips didn't move. "Or wings, perhaps?" He placed a palm on my father's still chest, using it as support to rise.

"Yes," I said, calmly. "I've seen what you can do. And you can't scare me anymore."

"No matter what you tell yourself, you will always be afraid." Blood dripped from the hand he'd placed on my father's body. His other hand still held the pistol he'd used to shoot my parents, and he now aimed it toward me. "You'll cut me free, then I'll make you fly."

"We're not in the tower anymore. Your threats are nothing but empty words."

Tarquin fired and the bullet went straight through my left shoulder. The momentum spun me halfway around, but I managed to remain standing. Blood splashed under my feet. More drained from the entrance wound. I bit my lip to suppress a scream.

"They were not empty words," he said in an

amused tone.

He was right. The pain was absolutely real... but the injury was not.

Like the rest of this place, the gunshot wound was an illusion—albeit a very convincing illusion. I focused on cutting through the illusion to see myself as I truly was and not what the simulation was showing me. It had less control over me than my surroundings.

Once I was able to see myself without the bleeding hole in my shoulder, the pain dissipated. And once the pain dissipated, the outer illusion adjusted to my experience, causing the wound to disappear from the simulation.

In the simulation, I'd managed to heal myself from a gunshot wound.

I returned my attention to Tarquin with a victorious grin. "Empty words," I said, confidently. "You can't hurt me." I had to believe the words—and I did.

His rage boiled over, and he unloaded all his remaining bullets on me.

I felt nothing. My body wasn't jostled with multiple impacts. The bullets sailed right through me as if I was nothing more than a ghost. And with the growing feeling of invincibility, I attacked.

I extracted the tip of my needle while teleporting to a spot directly behind Tarquin. As soon as I appeared, I swiped my needle across the air and through his back, separating the upper half of his body from the lower half by a glistening chasm of an open seam. Having learned from a previous mistake, I made two more gashes in the air, severing both of his arms as well. Tarquin was left as four floating sections and essentially rendered helpless.

"Fix me!" he roared, his body propped up by the sparkling blue seams I'd torn into the universal fabric.

The soles of my boots made sucking sounds in the congealing blood as I circled his body to confront him face-to-face. His face was nearly as red as the blood coating the ground. Fire filled his eyes. But as enraged as he was, he didn't have the power to touch me—physically or magically.

I stood close enough to feel the hot breath blowing from his flared nostrils, then proceeded to cut the red thread in his beard from which hairy black spiders dangled. I grabbed the severed threads and dropped the spiders into the blood. Most of them scurried away, but the ones that decided to stay were crushed underfoot.

"I will tear you limb from limb!" Tarquin bellowed, but the words now held no more substance then the ramblings of a crazy person.

I brought the tip of my needle extending from my forefinger to his face, which caused him to flinch. I moved it closer to his lips, then plucked at the red thread fusing his mouth shut. The string broke away with ease, barely requiring any pressure at all as I cut it all away, breaking the magical binding.

As soon as he opened his mouth, more spiders scurried out, nearly consuming the lower half of his face, causing me to jump back a few steps with a disgusted gasp. Soon, they were disappearing into his beard, taking the place of the spiders I'd previously cut free.

Tarquin coughed, and several more phlegm-covered spider projectiles shot straight at me.

I quickly manifested a fireball that consumed the incoming arachnids. They dropped into the blood pool with a flaming splat.

"Are you done?" I asked, still convinced to keep my distance. "I cut you free, just like you always wanted."

"Now stitch me back together," he demanded.

"That was never part of the request," I said with a smirk, then took the empty pistol from his useless hand. He could only resist with words. I focused on there being one more bullet in the magazine before pulling back the slide and loading it into the chamber.

I pointed the barrel at his forehead and looked him dead in the eyes. "I am in control now," I growled and pulled the trigger.

Click.

I was initially disappointed when the gun didn't fire, but I quickly regrouped and concentrated harder. I pulled back the slide, chambered another round, aimed, and pulled the trigger.

Click.

No disappointment this time, just increased determination. I repeated the process while Tarquin's disassociated body parts remained suspended in midair, and this time the gun fired. The bullet hit him between the eyes, and as a line of blood dripped down the side of his nose, Tarquin's head silently slumped forward.

I did it! I actually did it!

A wave of emotion hit me harder than the bullet did earlier in the encounter. The stoic front I'd been upholding crumbled as exhaustion and emotional overwhelm took over. I dropped the gun. My eyes burned. In the real world I wouldn't be able to leave him like this, but the seams I'd created were as simulated as everything else around me.

I wiped away a few errant tears with the back of my hand as I knelt beside the simulated bodies of my parents. They looked so real, but I could finally see through the fantasy.

I reached for the necklace chains and pulled the dull, blue crystals from their mouths. My mother's eyes were open, staring blankly into space, so I gently closed her lids.

"Thank you," I said, not exactly sure whom I was saying it to. Them? Tarquin? The entire fabricated world? It really didn't matter. What mattered was the sense of accomplishment I felt. Only I could fully know and appreciate what I'd overcome.

"Safe house."

CHAPTER 30

I gathered my belongings from the mailbox-shaped locker—careful to remember my crystal this time. I didn't greet my friends with an exuberant tale of triumph, but a conservative yet confident smile to show them I was good.

Razielle was all smiles, and Erik was beaming with pride. Even Nym, who had gone into the simulation with the best attitude she'd had all year emerged with her head held high. We were all conquering demons, extinguishing fears, and kicking ass. If you'd told me after the first day of the trimester that this was how I'd feel a month later, I'd say there was no freakin' way.

"This calls for a celebration," Razielle said and took Nym by the arm. And to everyone's surprise—

probably even Nym's—she didn't pull away. "You better come to dinner with us."

"Toby and I will be there," Nym said with a smile. She showed her fangs, but she made it look much more sweet than sinister.

Even though our celebration consisted of dinner in the cafeteria, the most important thing was that we were all together, laughing and sharing stories again. After the month we'd endured—some things planned, some not—we needed a moment to collectively breathe.

Unfortunately, I couldn't quite share in the insouciance everyone else expressed. I'd gotten a huge win today, but once the adrenaline wore off, the recent things weighing me down returned like shadows after a parting of the clouds. I couldn't simply shake them.

I was surrounded by happy couples, which only reminded me of the empty spot at our table. I still didn't know how I felt about the current status of our relationship, but my heart ached for Devon just the same. Maybe I wasn't fair to him this morning. We could have taken more time to talk it out, even with me not having an abundance of time in the moment. And here it was, hours later, and I'd yet to return a single message.

Then I had the issue of the man who looked like Professor Speaks pursuing me and the damned omen I'd been given this morning, both things clouding my celebratory mood. I'd reached a mountain peak—an especially difficult one to climb—but I was standing in the middle of the range, staring out at countless peaks left to reach. We all did, all in the midst of uncomfortable growth with many mountains left to explore and conquer. The difference was, I couldn't take my eyes off the next climb. I was restless atop my current peak.

After dinner, we meandered back to Shadow Peaks Hall and claimed the section of the lounge nearest the fireplace. It wasn't long before our boisterous conversations convinced the small number of students using the room for studying to abandon the lounge for a quieter location. We pulled chairs from around the room to create a semi-circle around the crackling fire.

Professor Ocumulus was summoned by our echoing voices after an hour or so, who insisted we break up the party and call it a night. We worked together to return the lounge to its original configuration, then most of us headed back to our respective rooms. Toby and Nym ventured outside to prolong their night a little longer.

"I have a moment of dread each time I come back to the room, waiting to see if there will be more nasty comments," Razielle said once we were safely inside. "I can't say that in front of Nym."

"I feel the same way since whoever did it is still out there, blending in with the crowd," I said. I plopped down on my bed to unlace and kick off my Docs. "However, I'd love to catch the asshole red handed."

"I bet you would," Razielle laughed. "And I'd love to see it." She tapped the side of the ladder a few times before climbing to the upper bunk. The boards creaked as she settled onto her mattress. "Man, I don't feel like finishing my homework. Maybe I'll get up early to do it."

Now, it was my turn to laugh. "That's something *I'd* love to see."

"I could do it… if I really wanted to."

"Great. Then do it."

"Maybe I will," she retorted.

I walked over to the wardrobe to retrieve my toiletry bag and begin my nightly routine. I wanted to get this stuff done early, so I could try and get a good night's sleep, then see how I felt about contacting Devon in the morning. No use in getting into an in-depth conversation—*or argument*—now because I'd never get to sleep.

It was relatively early, so the bathroom was nearly empty as I washed off my makeup and brushed my teeth. I exchanged pleasantries with the girl who washed her hands in the sink next to mine, but nothing more. She had her own group of friends, and I had mine. I took her for a nice girl, but over the past few years, I'd paid her very little attention.

As another couple of girls entered the bathroom,

I gathered my things, smiled to them, and returned to my room. When I got back, I could hear the soft hum of music coming from Razielle's earbuds. She was still out of view on the top bunk. I placed my toiletry bag back on the top shelf of my wardrobe. Then I removed my necklace but paused a moment to gaze upon the soul crystal before stowing it under a pile of folded jeans.

"I own you now," I said to myself, cupping my hand around the crystal. "Your hold over me is gone."

"You talking to me?" Razielle yelled, obviously music still playing in her ears.

"No, just to myself," I said, not removing my gaze from the blue crystal. It remained dark and cold.

What? You've got nothing to say to me? I moved the conversation into my head. *I beat you today, you son of a bitch. And I'll beat you every day from this point on until you fucking disappear.*

I closed my hand around the crystal, which remained cold. When I uncovered the crystal again, it was still just as dark and lifeless as an empty one.

It wasn't like Tarquin to ignore me. The power of the crystal was bright and palpable when he was upset—which was often the case. His rage fueled the crystal, and the power of the crystal fueled me.

Then the passing thought of an empty crystal sent a shiver through my body.

Clearly, there were ways to see the soul of

someone in the crystal—to even be able to fully communicate with the trapped soul—but it wasn't something I knew how to do. But I didn't need the specific skill to realize something was wrong.

My gut told me I was holding an empty crystal. And when I inspected it more closely, I noticed slight differences in the necklace and crystal, proving that this empty soul crystal wasn't mine. Despite the frustration, I was relieved to know that this wasn't my crystal and Tarquin had not been freed. Somehow my necklace had been switched…

…and there was only one time during the day when I took it off—one place where I was required to remove it.

What the hell?

I stuffed the empty crystal necklace in my jeans pocket and grabbed my Docs.

I didn't want to alarm Razielle, but wanted someone to know where I was headed, just in case. "I forgot my necklace in Combative Casting. I'll be right back," I said.

"Okay," Razielle said from the top bunk.

I left the room casually but rushed down the hallway and down the stairs. When I reached the basement, it was eerily quiet, my heavy footsteps echoing my thundering heart.

Only a few emergency lights were on inside the classroom. The door was locked. I liked the thought of slipping in and out unnoticed. But if the necklace had been deliberately taken from me, then there was a good chance it wasn't actually here but taken somewhere else.

I'd been challenged to search for my necklace before by connecting with Tarquin's soul and being guided by his energy. It had been over a year ago. I'd found the necklace beneath the Manor.

I closed my eyes and reached out to Tarquin, searching for the familiar sense of anger and hatred he felt for my family and me. And I was surprised to feel it almost immediately. The level of hatred emanating from the crystal was unmistakable. I wouldn't have to be dragged across campus, the crystal was still here.

I first tried to undo the magical lock, but it wouldn't turn.

Luckily, my needle made getting through locked doors just as easy. I extracted the tip of the needle and slid it down the face of the door. The glass and wood tore like paper, and after a large enough gash, I stepped into the classroom unrestrained. When I turned to check on the door, it had returned to its fully solid structure.

I scanned the classroom from where I stood, listening closely for any sounds from deeper inside the room. All the monitor screens at the computer station were dark except one, which flashed a regularly changing screensaver.

Convinced I was alone, I first hurried to my pod

to check the locker. I bent down to peer inside, only to find it empty. However, I sensed my crystal was close—the energy emanating from it nearly as strong as if I was wearing it.

Then I noticed the blue glow from inside my simulator pod. As I stood staring into the chamber, the blue glow brightened. I felt Tarquin's rage. He knew what I'd accomplished today, and he was pissed. I only wished I'd realized what I'd been missing earlier. Then I wouldn't be down here after hours, in the dark, with the dreaded question of what the hell was my necklace doing here? Someone had deliberately put it here... and that someone had lured me here as well.

I needed to get out of here, but couldn't leave without my necklace. I needed Tarquin in my possession. I needed the necklace.

I scanned the room again, and still I noticed no one and heard nothing.

Grab the necklace and run.

So, that's what I did. I dashed into the pod and reached for the necklace—only to stop when my fingers were inches from my desired possession.

The last time I'd found my necklace beneath the Manor, I'd touched it and had been immediately transported into the catacombs, where I was officially introduced to the plague vampires for the first time.

Shit!

I couldn't bring myself to touch the necklace out of the sudden fear it could've been hexed again, transformed into another portal that would transport me to only God knew where.

I stood, unsure of what to do next. Maybe if I picked it up with something, so I wouldn't touch it directly.

You need to get out of here, Rhodes! Something is definitely wrong!

And as I fought with myself over my next move, the door to the pod slid shut.

CHAPTER 31

I ran to the section of curved wall where the door had been, and banged against the impenetrable material.

"Let me out!" I screamed just as the world around me melted into a simulation. My eyes were open during the transition, which gave me a sense of vertigo and complete disorientation. I stumbled a few steps in open space before toppling to a stone floor.

I wasn't in the safe house. I'd been instantly returned to the lonely tower. And as my eyes adjusted to my new surroundings, I noticed the falling snow of feathers and broken wings littering the floor.

Oh God, what the hell is happening?

I tried not to panic, trying to convince myself that I'd been here before. I could handle whatever was thrown at me. I'd defeated Tarquin earlier today, and I could damn well do it again.

The necklace had been on the floor of the pod, but in the simulation, I could no longer see it. However, maybe it could be the key to getting out of here. If it truly was hexed, and it transported me out of here, maybe I'd have a better advantage.

Instead of getting to my feet, I crawled around on the floor, feeling for the necklace currently invisible to me. Even though I couldn't see it, the necklace was still there in the real world.

"There's my little bird," a sinister voice said from somewhere behind me.

I looked back and found Tarquin standing tall with a dismembered wing in one hand, blood still dripping from the bony stump.

The sight was horrifying, but my body no longer produced the visceral response it once had. I was slowly becoming desensitized to the nightmare I'd witnessed in my first year at the academy.

"I killed you once today," I said. "And I have no qualms about doing it again." My legs were a little shaky, but still managed to rise.

Before either of us committed to an attack, a vicious roar sounded—behind me on the other side of the circular room.

I knew exactly who was here.

The werewolf, the same one from the previous lonely tower encounter.

I turned halfway to keep both opponents in my periphery, then backed up a few steps to form a rough isosceles triangle. The wolfman was more focused on Tarquin than me, almost as if he remembered their battle from last time.

A deep growl rumbled from the werewolf's throat just before he sprang on Tarquin. Fireballs flying at the unnatural two-legged canine didn't slow him down a bit. When he collided with Tarquin, the two beasts crashed to the floor in a tangle of striking limbs.

I didn't know which one to root for.

If only they'd kill each other, but I doubted I'd be so lucky.

The wolfman snapped its large jaws, trying desperately to take a large bite out of Tarquin. So far, he was managing to hold the creature at bay, but I was noticing him already starting to tire. Those wicked teeth inched closer to Tarquin's face by the second. Then there was a snap, Tarquin's arm gave out, and the werewolf sank its teeth into the bearded man's face—almost able to fit his whole head in his massive jaws. More crunching as bones were crushed, skin was torn, and blood seeped down the side of Tarquin's head.

The lower part of his body was still kicking away, desperate to get out from under the humanoid creature. But as the wolfman continued to crush

Tarquin's head, the fight in the rest of his body steadily dissipated.

I didn't want to censor myself by looking away, no matter how graphic and sickly the scene became. Tarquin's fate was well deserved, and I owed it to myself to watch him die—over and over, if necessary.

When his body went still, it was almost a relief—until it occurred to me that I now had to face the victor.

The wolfman stood, leaving Tarquin's head in ruins. Now, he noticed me.

His jaws glistened with Tarquin's blood. He stalked toward me with a fiendish intensity, causing me to back into one of the stone ledges. The wind flowing through the open window was bitter cold. When I glanced over my shoulder, I noticed fog below, completely covering the ground. It looked as if we were in a tower above the clouds.

I quickly returned my attention to the approaching werewolf, and already, he was nearly upon me. I slid over to the left, so there would be stone at my back before shooting a volley of green energy balls to slow the monster's advance. I had no intention of being thrown out the window.

However, the wolfman barreled through my flaming projectiles as though they were nothing more than the feathers raining down from the ceiling. He slashed at me with a clawed hand, knocking me to the ground and causing me to cry out in pain. The points at the ends of his fingers were sharp as knives and cut through my clothes and skin just as easily.

As he stood over me, ready for another attack, I concentrated on getting out of the way. It took an extra few seconds, but I managed to teleport to a spot behind him. I called forth my needle and slashed at the air, but the creature disappeared just as suddenly. The next thing, I was being thrown. Crashing to the stone floor hurt like hell, but it was even worse as I rolled over bony wings that dug into my back, sides, and stomach.

When I regained my bearings, I suddenly noticed the whole world had changed. I was no longer in the simulated lonely tower, but back in the sterile white pod.

Everything had disappeared but one... the werewolf was still standing over me with snarling jaws that no longer dripped blood. Tarquin's blood had been an illusion. However, when I looked down at myself, I realized my blood was very much real.

This thing was inside the pod with me during the simulation! It had been here the whole time!

I was ready to slash at the wolfman with my needle again, but it caught my wrist before I was able to move as though it knew what I intended to do.

It looked closely at the needle sticking out of my finger, studying it inquisitively.

I knew I had to protect it at all costs, so I willed it to retract, making it look as though my finger was reabsorbing the needle.

The wolfman clumsily reached for the needle with two clawed fingers, but the needle slipped away before the creature managed to grab hold. It roared in frustration and squeezed my wrist so tightly, I thought it might snap.

"Did you get it?" a male voice asked from behind me.

I flinched at the sudden sound and was even more surprised to find Elliott standing in the doorway of the pod.

"No," the wolfman said in a brusque voice. "She will require more work."

I didn't like anything about this situation, but especially didn't like the sound of his words.

"She's been ranking really high on the simulations," Elliott said. "She's tough and will be a tough nut to crack."

"Tough is a relative term," the wolfman said. "Everything and everyone has a breaking point."

"Who are you?" I asked, knowing this was the creature who'd attacked Devon and me in the clearing. Was it the mysterious man who was also pursuing me? "Are you Professor Speaks?"

My question got a throaty chuckle from the

MICHAEL PIERCE

menacing monster still holding tightly to my wrist as I lay on the floor of the simulator pod. And he answered my question by transforming into the man I equated with Professor Speaks right before my eyes. I could finally see him in the light. His facial features were sharp, his cheeks unshaven. His short hair was straight but jutted out wildly in several directions as if he'd just pulled his hood off. He was dressed all in black and the hood on his fully zipped jacket was down. As the headmistress had said, he wasn't a shifter. His werewolf form was an illusion— though it had appeared as real as the simulation.

"Does this answer your question?" he asked.

He still gripped my wrist, continuing to keep me tethered to him. His hold on me was just as ironclad. When I glanced at his hand, I noticed short, but seriously sharp nails he'd enacted as claws. They'd been real—real enough to tear my clothing and draw blood.

It did, but I couldn't bring myself to answer. How was he here right now—in my simulation pod? How was he on campus with the increased security? What did he want with me?

I couldn't let the stream of questions running through my head distract me. I needed to focus on getting the hell out of here, which was what I should have done initially. My crystal was still on the floor behind Professor Speaks—the beacon that had lured me in here.

I teleported out of the professor's grasp, appeared behind him, and bent down to grab my soul crystal. And as I transitioned out of the room, he snatched me from the fade and pulled me back in.

"Not so fast," he said, grabbing my arm and hurling me toward the open door, forcing Elliott to leap out of the way to avoid a collision. "Keep her from escaping."

Before I had a chance to recover, Elliott grabbed my right wrist with one hand, then my precious forefinger with the other. He forcefully bent my finger and twisted it way out of its range of motion. I bit my lip and whimpered at the sound of the sickening snap and the wave of pain to follow. It took everything I had inside me not to scream.

Elliott let my arm drop, and I instantly cradled it with my good hand.

"Go ahead and try to teleport again," Professor Speaks challenged, squatting beside me with a devious grin. "Not so easy, is it? The pain compromises your concentration. Have you learned to heal yourself?"

I stared at him with a furious intensity, refusing to answer his seemingly casual questions.

"I thought not." He chuckled. "Unless you were taught outside the academy, it isn't covered until your fourth year." The professor reached back for my crystal. "However, you do have a soul crystal, even though I'm told you're a third year. You look older than the typical sapient. I'm sure your story is fascinating. Luckily, we'll have plenty of time to get better acquainted."

Professor Speaks dangled the crystal in front of me, making it swing to and fro like a sparkling blue pendulum. I couldn't take my eyes off it. As I focused on the gem, my pain subsided... but so did my awareness of the room in which I precariously sat on the floor.

"Sweet dreams, seamstress," he said in a deeply calming voice, the only sound left in the world. "We'll talk again soon."

AFTER THE FINAL WORD

FEBRUARY 18, 2022

I first and foremost want to thank you for reading *Sapient Curse*, and now you're even continuing with the author's note! I'm so grateful and could obviously not do this without you.

This book has been a long time coming. After *Chrysalis*, I took a slight detour to finish my *Angeles Vampire* series, for which I had two books left to write. Once they were finished, I jumped back into Spellcrest to start the third story arc—Maeve and the gang's sapient year.

I finished the *Angeles Vampire* series, but transitioning back to Spellcrest wasn't as easy as I'd hoped. I started *Sapient Curse* nearly a year ago. Some days the words just flowed (how us authors always want them to), and other days I couldn't even bring myself to sit at my computer. Many of those frustrating days unintentionally stretched into weeks.

When that happens, momentum gets lost, and it's an uphill battle to get it back.

At that time in early 2021, we were all bracing ourselves for the second year of the pandemic, with the horizon not moving any closer. I was emotionally drained with life, and my writing suffered as a result.

However, I didn't quit. This was the longest it has ever taken me to write a book. Even my first book took me less time, which is saying something. There were days I wanted to throw in the towel and scream, "I'm done!"

But I managed to get through those days and slowly add more words to the manuscript. If you don't give up, you can't fail. So, I persisted. Not from finding some divine inspiration, but through shear will, determination, and a sense of obligation.

As a result, I'm very proud with how the book ultimately came out. I can only hope, the next book won't take nearly as long—that I can get back to my pre-pandemic writing rhythm. And to provide extra motivation, I've already put the next book on pre-order, so I can't take another year! The power of a deadline to provide a real kick in the ass!

No one likes being left dangling from a cliffhanger for too long. I understand and fully appreciate that. So, I'll continue to work hard to get the next book in your hands as quickly as possible (or sanity will allow). And with that being said, I better get back to work!

As always, if you enjoyed this book, then please leave a review, and tell your friends and the strangers standing in line with you at Starbucks (or insert your favorite coffee shop here). Reviews and word of mouth are the best ways to support authors you love.

Thank you again, and I look forward to seeing you in the next story.

Onward,
   Michael Pierce

How would you like to read an exclusive Bonus Chapter for *Sapient Curse* that you cannot get anywhere else? It provides an exciting continuation of the story you just finished—a little insider information for true fans.

If you're not already a member of my newsletter, then you'll also be the first to hear about my new releases, promotions, giveaways, and other fun stuff intended to lift your spirits.

What are you waiting for? Your *Sapient Curse* exclusive Bonus Chapter awaits...

Download your Bonus Chapter now:
https://www.michaelpierceauthor.com//spellcrest-academy-signup

Royal Replicas (Book 1)

Royal Captives (Book 2)

Royal Threat (Book 3)

Royal Return (Book 4)

THE HIGHER REALMS SERIES (*Complete*)

Provex City Box Set

Provex City (Book 1)

SUSY Asylum (Book 2)

Doria Falls (Book 3)

Archanum Manor (Book 4)

ABOUT THE AUTHOR

Michael Pierce is a young adult author of urban fantasy, paranormal romance, and sci-fi dystopian. His books are thrilling and unexpected, romantic and fantastical—addictive tales sure to keep you reading long past the witching hour.

Michael currently lives in Southern California with his wife, two children, and attention-craving chiweenie.

Connect with him online:
michaelpierceauthor.com
michael@michaelpierceauthor.com

Printed in Great Britain
by Amazon

81345680R00192